"After you're in the h
be additional shopp

For what?" Edmond asked.

Curtains, for one thing. As I recall, the blinds in that house provide privacy but they aren't decorative."

Oh, right." While he'd considered the cost of child care, he hadn't factored in yard care. "And a cleaning service, too. Any recommendations?"

We clean our own house, so I'm not sure. Just ask at work. You'll be inundated with suggestions." She was grinning widely.

What's so funny?"

You're usually on top of every situation." She slipped her pad into a pocket. "It's refreshing to see you out of your element."

Refreshing?" That wasn't the word Edmond would have chosen. "Awkward, maybe. Embarrassing."

No, it's cute." She'd never called him that before. "Human."

As opposed to my usual robotic self?" he asked.

In a sense," she teased. "It's fun to watch the ice melt."

He traced her temple with his thumb. "Only with you." Her radiance drew him in, drew him close. He tilted his head, longing for her, but holding back.

And then, as if it were the most natural thing in the world, she looped her arms around his shoulders and kissed him....

Dear Reader,

Welcome to Safe Harbor, and please don't worry if you haven't read all—or any—of the previous books, because each stands alone. Each also presents unique challenges to me as a writer.

When I sketched the storyline for this book, I had no idea how much research the writing would entail. Some of it was already in my files, such as background on embryo transfers and multiple pregnancies. And I had some experience in court matters, having helped cover several trials for the Associated Press and having served on a jury.

However, I soon realized I needed to understand the special needs of children whose parents are sent to prison; how to arrange for such a child's guardianship so she doesn't end up in the foster care system, and how the sentencing would unfold in a courtroom.

I'm grateful for the internet, a gold mine of information. When the internet doesn't suffice, however, I seek out experts to interview. Luckily, I have a friend who's a Superior Court judge and who explained to me what goes on when a sentence is handed down, as in the case of Edmond's sister.

My goal is to weave in the background so smoothly that it supports rather than interferes with the emotions of the story. I hope I've succeeded. Happy reading!

Best,

Jacqueline Diamond

THE SURPRISE TRIPLETS

JACQUELINE DIAMOND

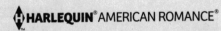
HARLEQUIN® AMERICAN ROMANCE®

Recycling programs
for this product may
not exist in your area.

ISBN-13: 978-0-373-75536-3

THE SURPRISE TRIPLETS

Copyright © 2014 by Jackie Hyman

Printed in U.S.A.

www.Harlequin.com

ABOUT THE AUTHOR

Medical themes feature prominently among Jacqueline Diamond's more than 95 published novels, especially her Safe Harbor Medical miniseries for Harlequin American Romance. Delivered at home by her physician father—the only doctor in their small Texas town—Jackie moved with her parents and brother to Louisville, Kentucky, and later Nashville, Tennessee. She developed an interest in fertility issues after successfully undergoing treatment to have her two sons, now in their twenties. Her books include Regency romances, romantic intrigues, romantic comedies and mysteries. A former Associated Press reporter and columnist, she lives with her husband of thirty-five years in Orange County, California, where she's active in Romance Writers of America. You can see an overview of the Safe Harbor Medical miniseries at www.jacquelinediamond.com and say hello to Jackie at her Facebook page, JacquelineDiamondAuthor.

Books by Jacqueline Diamond

HARLEQUIN AMERICAN ROMANCE

For Kevin and Renée Brown, two very special friends

Chapter One

The man and woman sitting in front of Melissa Everhart's desk held hands as if about to jump off a cliff together. In a sense, that *was* what they were doing.

Be careful what you wish for, she wanted to caution them. But in her role as Safe Harbor Medical Center's *in vitro* fertilization and egg donor coordinator, she was already providing them with full information. Any further warning would be an unprofessional insertion of her personal concerns.

"Most people who hire a surrogate and can't provide their own eggs prefer to use a separate egg donor," she was explaining.

"Why bring in a third party?" The woman, Bev Landry, an accountant in her early forties, projected a professional image in her tailored gray suit with a rose-colored silk blouse. Only the clenched hands in her lap betrayed her nervousness as she and her husband embarked on an expensive and by-no-means-guaranteed quest to have a child via surrogacy. An ovarian cancer survivor, she had tried to adopt without success.

Bev longed for a baby with all her heart. Melissa understood that yearning because she'd shared it.

"I'm not a lawyer, but I can tell you that while surrogates—or gestational carriers, as they're termed—sign away their rights to the baby, it's still safer legally and emotionally if there's no genetic link," Melissa informed her.

"That brings up the issue of legalities..." Bev's husband, Mick, a rough-hewn building contractor, leaned forward aggressively. It was, Melissa judged, merely his way of taking control of a scary situation. "What protection do we have when we commission—if that's the right word—a child?"

"We're fortunate that California leads the world in safeguarding your rights," she said. "I have several documents here on the subject, including new laws and court decisions favoring the designated parents."

Mick glanced at the documents she handed him, then set them aside for later. "Thanks. And I'll be the biological father, after all."

"That's right. Now let's talk about how you would select your egg donor and your surrogate." Although the hospital's brochures covered all aspects of its fertility program, the information could be overwhelming. It was Melissa's job to steer clients through the process.

If she deemed it advisable, she could also refer them to the hospital's psychologist. And, starting today, she could offer them a free session with the hospital's new consulting family attorney. Who just happened to be her ex-husband.

Her throat tightened. A year ago, without explanation, her ex-husband Edmond had given up a high-paying position in Los Angeles to join a tiny law firm here in Safe Harbor. Then, a month or so ago, he'd applied for a consulting job at the hospital. Despite her reservations, when the administrator had asked Melissa whether bringing Edmond on board in a part-time position would pose problems for her, she'd said no.

His new job meant they might occasionally have to work together, but since their divorce three years ago, they'd remained on civil terms. She respected Edmond's abilities and had always found him easy to confer with.

Except on one issue. Edmond had vehemently opposed having children. Initially, Melissa hadn't wanted them, either, but she'd changed her mind during their five-year marriage. As her thirtieth birthday approached, her longing for little ones to love had intensified to the point that she could no longer ignore it.

Hesitantly, she'd brought up with her husband the possibility of having kids. Edmond hadn't taken it well, and to her shock, he'd then gone out and had a vasectomy without consulting her. Stunned by this high-handed maneuver and devastated that he thought so little of her needs, Melissa had left him.

The man she'd believed was her true love had turned out to be fatally flawed. Unfortunately, her post-divorce attempts at finding another Mr. Right had led nowhere.

Now she was going it alone, she reflected as her hand drifted to her abdomen, where it felt as if she had a watermelon strapped to her midsection. No telling how Edmond would react when he saw her condition. But then, he'd made his choice, and she'd made hers.

She trained her attention on the computer screen and angled it toward the Landrys. "We provide photographs and profiles of our surrogates, as we do with egg donors in a separate registry. You'll have your own code to sign onto our secure website from home...." As Melissa spoke, she heard a flurry of noises outside the closed door. Hers was one of four offices opening off the fertility support program's reception area on the hospital's ground floor. Judging by the scuff of footsteps and the warm tones of her colleagues, she guessed that the hospital administrator was introducing the new consultant.

Then a deep, familiar voice rumbled through her. Melissa's skin prickled. *Edmond.* If only she wasn't still so sensitized to his nearness. Maybe agreeing for him to join the staff had been a mistake. Too late to change her mind now.

"Oh, my goodness!" Bev tugged an ultrasound photo from beneath a few papers on the desk. "Is that twins? No, there's a third one. Triplets! Incredible."

Her husband craned his neck to study the image. "Somebody hit the jackpot."

Melissa's cheeks heated. "I shouldn't have left that in view."

"I'm sorry." Bev set down the image. "I didn't mean to invade anyone's privacy. That woman is so lucky!"

Is she? "Actually, it's me."

Bev's mouth flew open. "Seriously? I noticed you were pregnant but I had no idea it was triplets. How far along are you?"

"Four months down, five to go." According to Melissa's obstetrician, multiple births usually resulted in early deliveries, but she was trying to think positively.

"Your husband must be excited," Mick said.

Melissa tilted her head in a half nod and hoped he wouldn't notice her failure to respond further. "Do you have questions about what we've discussed so far?"

"Once we've chosen the surrogate, how many fertilized eggs would be implanted?" Mick said. "I mean, assuming more than one is usable."

"That can be a difficult decision," she told him. "Multiple pregnancies are risky. On the other hand, only implanting one embryo lowers the odds of success. In the U.K. and Australia, doctors are limited by law to transferring a maximum of two embryos."

He scowled. "Are there any restrictions in California?"

"No." Trying to ignore the increasingly loud chatter from the outer office, she said, "However, our doctors limit themselves to implanting a maximum of three embryos, for medical and ethical reasons."

"But the embryos won't all attach, right?" Bev asked.

"Not usually." She certainly hadn't expected them to. "Twins or singletons are much more common than triplets."

From the outer office came the squeal of the high-spirited receptionist, Caroline Carter. "I had no idea you were Melissa's ex-husband!"

Melissa winced.

Edmond replied in a low tone, something about "good terms." All the same, Melissa's face was flaming. "Sorry for the disturbance," she said to the Landrys.

"No need to apologize," said Mick. "We're the ones who changed our appointment at the last minute." They'd been scheduled to meet with her in the afternoon.

"It didn't occur to me that this might overlap. We have a new legal consultant at the hospital." At a tap on the door, Melissa started to rise. When her abdominal muscles protested, she put a hand on the desktop for support.

"Please don't exert yourself. I'll get it." Uncoiling from his chair, Mick crossed the floor. Since he was closer, she yielded without protest.

Melissa braced for this encounter with Edmond. They'd run into each other occasionally since he'd arrived in town and they'd exchanged polite how-are-yous. He'd represented one of her housemates in a divorce, and another, briefly, on a custody issue. She'd assured her friends that he was an excellent attorney, which was true. But this was her home territory.

Just say hello and it'll be over. For now. And if she remained seated, she might be able to save her startling news until they were alone.

Mick opened the door. "Don't mind me. I'm the butler," he joked to the imposing administrator, Dr. Mark Rayburn, a large man with black hair and power eyebrows.

"Pardon the interruption," Mark said. "We have a new attorney on staff and today's his first chance to meet everybody. We'll just be a sec."

"No problem." Extending his hand, Mick introduced himself and his wife.

The slim, strong man Melissa had once loved moved past Mark, and cool brown eyes met hers from behind steel-framed glasses. It was lucky that her clients were comfortable chatting with the newcomers, because her voice got stuck in her throat.

As always, her ex-husband was impeccably groomed—even in July, he wore a jacket and tie. Being in the same room made her keenly aware of his light, spicy scent and the breadth of his chest.

And it also made her aware of how much she missed curling against him at night, missed talking over the day's events and missed his logical insights. Once, she could have tracked his reactions to people and events as easily as her own. It was disorienting, to have no idea what he was thinking right now.

What was wrong with her? It must be the emotional effect of maternal hormones. She'd long ago resolved any lingering sense that she belonged with this man.

"Good to see you, Melissa." He sounded slightly hoarse.

"You, too," she managed. She ought to rise, but if she did...

At Mark's subtle prompting, Edmond greeted the Landrys and handed them his business card. "If you have any legal questions, I'd be happy to schedule a free consultation here at the hospital. I have office hours Monday mornings and Thursday afternoons."

"Maybe later," Mick said. "We're still in the early stages."

The administrator indicated they should move on. Just when Melissa figured the encounter was over, Edmond swung toward her. "Okay if I stop by in a few minutes? There are a few matters we should discuss."

"Certainly." All very professional, although everybody

in the office—plus the cheerily nosy receptionist lingering outside the door—must be aware of the undercurrents.

When he held out his hand, there was no avoiding it. Melissa stood up, big belly and all.

Edmond's jaw dropped and his body went rigid. His double take might almost have been comical, had she not felt his shock so keenly. Melissa had prepared herself for his disapproval or anger, or perhaps indifference. To her surprise, she caught a glint of pain.

His gaze went to her left hand, to her ringless third finger. But he could hardly draw conclusions from that. Pregnant women often removed their wedding rings to accommodate puffiness.

He cleared his throat. "I'll talk to you later, then. Nice to meet you, Mr. and Mrs. Landry."

As Mark ushered Edmond out, he regarded Melissa with concern. He didn't miss much, she reflected, and she smiled in an attempt to reassure him.

With a nod, the big man closed the door. She hadn't fooled him. She wasn't fooling anybody these days, except maybe herself. *Oh, quit overthinking this.*

The Landrys resumed their seats and Melissa did the same. Returning to their discussion, she said, "You might try listing the qualities that are most important to you in an egg donor and a surrogate. That will guide your choices."

Her suggestion had the desired effect of pushing the interruption from their minds. When the clients departed a quarter of an hour later, Melissa had recovered her equilibrium.

She reached for her cup of tea, to find it empty. Although an hour remained until lunch, she was starving, and she'd already finished off the crackers in her desk. These days, she found herself eating more than enough for four. Her doctor insisted her weight gain was healthy, but Melissa had trouble adjusting to her rotund body shape. At five-foot-eight, she'd always been tall and slender.

Well, she was still tall.

The slightly open door swung wider, and she forgot to breathe. Then she saw with relief that her visitor wasn't Edmond.

Karen Wiggins, the fertility program's financial counselor and occupant of the adjacent office, handed her a cup of white liquid. "It's almond milk—fifty percent more calcium than cow's milk."

"Thanks, Mom," Melissa teased. Ten years her senior, Karen was a nurturing friend as well as her landlady.

"How'd it go with the ex?" Karen lingered near the desk. This month, she'd dyed her shoulder-length hair reddish-brown, which Melissa preferred to some of her friend's more flamboyant choices.

"Smoothly. Oddly. I don't know." Staying alert for approaching footsteps, Melissa added, "He'll be back any minute."

"I'll talk fast. Did you pay attention to the guest list for Saturday?"

"No. Should I?" Melissa and three other coworkers rented rooms in Karen's large home. This weekend, one of their group, nurse Anya Meeks, was getting married there. "As long as we have enough food, who cares?"

"You don't mind that Edmond's invited?"

That was a less-than-welcome surprise. "I had no idea. I wasn't aware he knew Anya and Jack that well."

Karen shrugged. "Anya posted on her wedding website that he'd brought them together. You'll recall she hired him to arrange for Jack to waive his paternal rights after she found out she was pregnant. That set off a whole chain of events leading to…" She hummed a few bars of "Here Comes the Bride."

"Oh, that's right." Several months ago, Anya had asked

about a lawyer to help her explore giving up her baby for adoption and Melissa had recommended Edmond. "That hardly qualifies him as Cupid." She sipped the milky liquid, enjoying its slight vanilla flavor.

"She led me to believe she'd already told Jack about the pregnancy." Edmond peered through the doorway, his brown eyes alight with amusement at slipping into the discussion. "I dropped off what I assumed was routine paperwork to Jack and—bam! Fireworks."

Despite an instinctive tensing at his appearance, Melissa had to smile at the image of her normally unflappable ex-husband facing Jack's outrage. "You smoothed things over."

"Not entirely. It was among the more awkward moments of my career," Edmond said. "But all's well that ends well."

"And you're coming to my house on Saturday?" Karen asked.

He gave a start. "The wedding's at your house?"

"The address is on the invitation," Karen pointed out.

"I didn't check where it was. I figured I'd GPS it." A puzzled line formed between Edmond's dark eyebrows. "By the way, why did the invitation come with nose clips?"

Both women laughed. "You'll find out," Karen said.

Aware that Edmond disliked being kept in the dark, Melissa explained, "The house is next to an estuary. The smell of decomposing vegetation and fish can get a little ripe."

"Dare I hope the wedding's indoors?" he asked. "Nose clips don't work too well with glasses."

"It is," she assured him.

"Glad to hear it."

Karen scooped up Melissa's empty mug. "Later, guys." Then she left them alone.

Chapter Two

Edmond's ethics had prevented him from questioning fellow staffers about his ex-wife's pregnancy. Now that they were in private, though, it took all his resolve not to blurt the questions bedeviling him.

How frustrating that her condition made her glow even more than usual. That was saying a lot. The first time he'd seen Melissa, sitting with her friends at a UCLA campus coffee shop, light through a leaded glass window had bathed her in gold. Now, at the memory, her radiance hit him doubly hard.

They'd been a couple from the moment they met. He'd opened up to her, and she to him, or so he'd believed. They'd agreed that their marriage, their intimacy and their commitment would always be the center of their lives.

He'd been frank about the fact that fatherhood, on top of his demanding profession, would bring too many pressures. Edmond did nothing halfway, and he understood how important a father was to his children—a loving, devoted father, not a man who had them just because others expected him to. He'd taken on family responsibilities too young, filling in with his younger sister for an often-absent father and an emotionally withdrawn mother. And had done a poor job with her, as things turned out.

His wife's announcement after five years of marriage that she wanted children had come out of nowhere. No warning, no hints before then that she'd changed her mind. Astonished and angry, he'd reacted strongly. Perhaps too strongly, but surely they could have saved their marriage if she was open to it. Instead, she'd walked out and cut off all communication about everything except divorce.

Despite his resentment, their deep connection had lingered in Edmond's thoughts through the years. Although her presence in Safe Harbor hadn't been his only reason for moving here, he'd looked forward to reconnecting, at least on a friendship basis. A friendship that might, in time, have grown.

No chance of that now. Not that Edmond begrudged her happiness. "Pregnancy suits you."

Melissa's eyes widened in surprise. "Nice of you to say so."

"I never pay idle compliments."

"I'm aware of that." She waved him into a chair in front of her desk. A handful of brochures and papers were stacked more or less neatly on its polished wooden surface.

"Thank you for consenting to me being hired." He'd been pleased to learn from Dr. Rayburn that she'd raised no objection.

"You'll do a good job." Her tapered fingers started to drum the desk, then stopped. "Why do you wish to be a consultant here?"

Noting her tension, he wondered at it. If she'd fallen in love with someone new, surely she'd be indifferent to him. Also, if she loved the father of her child, why was she sharing a house with friends?

"I applied for the post for financial and professional reasons," he answered. "Until I arrived at Geoff Humphreys and Associates, the 'associates' consisted of a legal secretary and a receptionist. I'm slowly building a clientele, but it's going to take a while." He decided against mentioning that he'd also been attracted to the hospital opening because she was on staff.

"Why did you leave L.A.?" she asked. "I'm sure it paid better." He'd earned a hefty salary, plus bonuses.

"It was cutthroat." The partners at his old firm had encouraged associates to go for the jugular. The more Edmond saw of vicious divorces and custody battles, the less he appreciated that approach to family law.

Despite their pain, he and Melissa had behaved like rational adults during the divorce. That experience had been part of the reason he'd switched his focus to collaborative law and joined a smaller firm.

There'd been other reasons, as well. He'd sought to reduce his hours so he could help his parents and sister, who'd had a rough year. Then, after meeting Geoff and finding that their views dovetailed, he'd leaped at the chance to move to Safe Harbor. And possibly, to start over with Melissa.

Until today, he hadn't admitted to himself how much he'd hoped she'd let go of her desire to have children. Once, she'd valued being with him above everything else, and as the years passed and she hadn't remarried, he'd wondered if she might be experiencing some regret.

Obviously, he'd been wrong. Regardless of who the father was, she'd made an irreversible commitment to the child inside her. This pregnancy meant he'd truly lost her.

"So the short version is, you took the hospital consulting job because you need the business," Melissa summarized.

"Harsh but accurate," Edmond conceded. "Also, the legal aspects of new medical technologies present an interesting challenge."

She crossed her arms. "I don't view my clients' legal concerns as an 'interesting challenge.' They're individuals facing real-life issues." Judging by her tone, he gathered that he'd irritated her.

"Of course they're individuals, but when they consult a lawyer, they deserve objective advice more than hand-holding." Rather than continue in this vein, Edmond added, "My job description also includes educating the staff on family law topics, such as changes regarding adoptions and surrogacy."

"I presume Tony is on board with this."

"He's the one who requested they hire a consultant." Tony Franco, the hospital's regular attorney, had his hands full dealing with liability and malpractice matters, as well as refining policies on patient privacy, patient rights and the *in vitro* program. "Geoff introduced us on the golf course a few months ago. He suggested I apply for the opening."

"Congratulations." Melissa stopped there. Whatever she was thinking, she guarded it well. He used to consider her an open book, but then again, if that had been true, he'd have had some idea of how radically she'd altered her opinion of parenthood.

After a brief silence, he said, "Let's discuss how I can assist you with fertility patients. You're on the front lines, I understand."

"Fine. Later."

"Why not now?" He wasn't ready to cut short this meeting, not until he had a clearer picture of where she stood. How she felt. Who the damn father was.

Instead of a direct answer, she blurted, "Don't go to the wedding."

So that's what's on her mind. Edmond struggled to catch this conversational curve ball. "I already RSVP'd."

"It isn't set in concrete." A cord of tension stood out in her slender neck. "You're only attending to expand your contacts in the community, right?"

Not entirely. "There are personal as well as professional reasons. I had no idea it was at your house." Why did this bother her? She'd agreed to work with him.

"It's an informal event," Melissa said. "One person more or less won't affect anything. It's not as if Jack and Anya will be stuck paying a caterer for an uneaten meal."

Edmond had a tight schedule on Saturday, and skipping the afternoon event might ease things. But in view of his new consulting job, her friends were now his coworkers. Breaking his promise to attend would be rude. And he didn't understand her reluctance.

Was she trying to hide the circumstances of her pregnancy? Surely she didn't expect to keep him in the dark for long. Had she broken up with the father? Or was the prospect of introducing him to her ex-husband uncomfortable?

Edmond half hoped the guy was a bum with body odor. *Maybe that's the real reason for the nose clips.* At the ridiculous notion, he smiled.

"You find this funny?" she asked.

"I was just…" He shook off his reflections. "We live in the same community."

"Your choice, not mine." Her low tone bordered on a growl.

"You gave your permission," he reminded her.

"Not for you to relocate to Safe Harbor, only for this job. I've never been vindictive."

"That's true."

"Then do me a favor and…" Halting, she paled, and sucked in several quick breaths.

"Are you okay?" Edmond leaned across the desk. "Shall I call someone?"

"What I need is tea."

"I'll get it."

"Never mind."

This was ridiculous. "We aren't enemies," he said. "Melissa, tell me what I can do."

"I don't want your help." Were those tears in her eyes? "And it's just a touch of morning sickness. Gone already."

Perhaps, yet her distress troubled him. "You're sure?"

"Yes. And if I change my mind about the tea, I'll ask Caroline."

Damn, she was hardheaded. "Surely we can find common ground and give each other a break," he said. "I've been dealing with family matters...I could use your insights. And in your situation, you shouldn't be too quick to reject an offer of friendship."

He'd phrased that badly, he saw when her chin lifted defiantly. "I have plenty of friends. What do you mean by 'my situation,' anyway?"

"You haven't mentioned the father." Oh, hell, he was making matters worse. "Not that it's any of my business."

"There is no father."

She hadn't fallen in love with another man. That discovery brought some comfort, but Edmond also found it disturbing. How desperately she must want a child to undergo insemination by an anonymous donor.

She was awaiting a reaction to her statement. If she expected reassurances, he had to disappoint her. "Is that fair to the child? Fathers matter."

"I have guy friends," she told him. "Guys who think kids are precious."

"Friends aren't family." Nor did she have any other family, unfortunately. Her parents had died years ago, and her younger brother had drowned as a toddler.

"Lots of women raise children alone," Melissa flared.

Edmond was glad the color had returned to her cheeks, even though it was an angry red. "In any case, nothing I say matters. Your baby is your priority now."

"That's right."

They'd reached an impasse, and the end of this conversation. Edmond didn't offer to shake hands, which might force her to rise. "I'll see you on Saturday."

"You're determined to attend the wedding?" she asked tightly.

"As I said, I already accepted." If she could be stubborn, so could he. On the spur of the moment, he added, "I'll be bringing a plus one, by the way."

"Suit yourself." She faced her computer, dismissing him.

In the outer office, Edmond paused at Caroline Carter's desk. An attractive young woman with a smooth dark complexion and a romance novel partly visible on her lap, she regarded him brightly. "Yes, Mr. Everhart?"

"If you wouldn't mind, my... Melissa could use some tea. Her stomach's bothering her," he said.

"I'm on it," she responded. "And welcome to Safe Harbor."

"Glad to be here." He exited into the main-floor hallway, where he was engulfed by the chatter and bustle of personnel heading for the cafeteria. Despite the flat lighting and the smell of antiseptic, he liked this place. The air hummed with the enthusiasm of people dedicated to their work.

It had been a rocky meeting with his ex-wife. But they'd accomplished an important task: clarifying that they stood as far apart as ever.

EVERY MINUTE CLOSER to lunch, Melissa felt nearer to starvation, and today's cafeteria special had been posted as chicken enchiladas with guacamole, a favorite of hers. Nevertheless, her friends would spot her frayed emotional state the moment she sat at their table, and she wasn't ready to field questions.

Why was Edmond so stubborn about the wedding? And why had she overreacted? She hadn't intended to demand that he skip it.

When he'd observed that pregnancy suited her, a wall inside her had started to crumble, and his strong presence had reawakened a longing to lean on him. What an absurd idea, and yet he'd been her rock after her parents' sudden deaths in an accident, and she needed someone to talk to right now.

But when he'd pushed her away, it stung, revealing a vulnerability Melissa had believed long vanquished. How could she still have feelings for the man who'd broken her heart?

Considering his dismissive attitude toward fatherhood, he had a lot of nerve, criticizing her decision. *Is that fair to the child? Fathers matter.* As if she hadn't taken that into consideration.

In fact, she'd been reluctant to undergo artificial insemination. Melissa had questioned how she would explain to a child later that its father had no involvement, indeed no awareness of its existence.

Then a couple of *in vitro* clients to whom she'd grown close had faced a dilemma. After bearing healthy triplets, they'd been left with three unused embryos. Due to a difficult pregnancy and with three children to raise, they'd decided against another pregnancy. Instead, they'd resolved to donate the embryos.

Recalling an earlier conversation with Melissa, they'd offered the little ones to her. With her, they'd insisted, they wouldn't worry because they had confidence she'd be a wonderful mother. But they'd also been in a rush to settle the matter and told her if she didn't seize the chance immediately, they'd select another recipient.

Her physician, Dr. Zack Sargent, had noted the potential physical complications of a multiple pregnancy but, in view of her general good health, he'd given his approval. When she'd solicited the opinions of her housemates and a few dinner guests, Anya's fiancé, obstetrician Jack Ryder, had said that frozen embryo transfers at Safe Harbor had about a fifty percent success rate. That statistic reinforced Melissa's assumption that at most she'd bear twins.

She'd also received enthusiastic support from Karen. Divorced and in her early forties, her friend had no plans for children of her own but loved being around babies. Another housemate, male nurse Lucky Mendez, had advised Melissa to follow her heart instead of obsessing about everything that could go wrong. Only ultrasound technician Zora Raditch had been dubious, but then, Zora had accidentally become pregnant with twins after having breakup sex with her faithless ex-husband, so her opinion of men and maternity was understandably jaundiced.

It had felt like fate. Then all three embryos had taken. *And now here I am, hurting because the man I used to love won't accept me the way I am.* What a waste of energy.

Annoyed at her weakness, she picked up the phone and put in a call to Rose's Posies. As her wedding gift to Jack and Anya, she was providing the bouquets for the bride and for two flower girls, as well as for one of Anya's sisters, who was flying in from Colorado to serve as maid of honor.

The shop owner, Rose Nguyen, answered on the fourth ring. "I'll go check to be sure my daughter has all in order," she said after Melissa explained she was calling to confirm the arrangements. "Hold for Violet, okay?"

"Thanks." Melissa smiled at the name of Rose's daughter. Like her mother's, it was sweetly appropriate.

She stretched her legs, slipped off her pumps and rested her swollen feet on a stool beneath the desk while making a mental note to buy larger shoes. Preferably before Saturday, to go with the flowing silk caftan she'd found at the Gently Used & Useful thrift shop.

Heat flooded her at the realization that, flattering as the lavender print dress might be, it emphasized her girth. She'd been rather proud of that until Edmond mentioned bringing a date.

Who was it? The legal secretary or the receptionist from

his office, a friend from L.A., or a new acquaintance? She'd probably be pretty, smart and slim.

Melissa shook her head at her insecurities. *Take Lucky's advice. Stop obsessing.*

On the other end of the line, someone picked up. "Ms. Everhart?" It was Violet. "Let me review the order with you to be sure we have everything as you requested."

"Good idea."

A few minutes later, as they finished talking, Melissa's stomach quivered. No, that wasn't her stomach. She clamped her hand to her abdomen. The babies were moving. Although they'd been visibly active during a recent ultrasound, she hadn't been able to feel them.

Her tests had revealed three girls, but until now they'd remained figures on a screen. This fluttery sensation filled her with wonder. *My daughters are playing.*

Picking up the sonogram picture, she studied the tiny people until tears blurred her vision. They were helpless, utterly dependent on their lone parent. Sometimes the reality of her pregnancy and her future as a single mom to triplets was overwhelming, but she could do it.

Everyone believed in her ability to love and raise them—her friends, her coworkers and Nell and Vernon Grant, the couple who'd donated the embryos. Everyone except Edmond. Well, he was wrong, just as he'd been wrong three years ago.

As for how she'd compare on Saturday to whoever he was bringing to the wedding, why should she care? They'd spent five happy years together but, ultimately, he'd been the wrong man for her.

Still, it wouldn't hurt to stop by The Baby Bump on her way home. Perhaps the shop carried something more flattering than the billowy lavender dress.

Chapter Three

A white satin bow and a bouquet of red, white and blue balloons adorned the mailbox in front of the two-story house. Edmond didn't have to check the address as he wedged his black sedan into a space by the curb. Even had the decorations not identified this as the wedding site, it was the only residence along this stretch of Pelican Lane, bordering the salt marsh and ending half a block away at the Pacific Ocean. If there'd been other homes here in the past, they must have been bought up and removed to restore the estuary.

"Is this it?" His wedding date, her green eyes filled with uncertainty, regarded the rolling lawn and long gravel driveway packed with vehicles.

"We're here," he confirmed. As she unstrapped the belt that she'd carefully positioned to avoid wrinkling her party dress, Edmond reached for his door handle. The ground was soft, and he'd prefer to carry her rather than risk dirtying her sparkly shoes.

Although he'd been warned, he hadn't been prepared for the pungent smell that struck his nostrils the instant he stepped out. His date noticed, too, of course. As he swung her from her seat and around to the roadway, her nose wrinkled in disgust. "Pee-yoo."

"Want to borrow those nose clips?" He'd shown them to her earlier.

She gave him a gap-toothed smile. "That might leave red marks, Uncle Eddie."

"We can't have that!"

"A fairy princess has to look perfect," she agreed.

"And so you do." Taking her hand, he led seven-year-old Dawn along the street bordering the yard. There was no sidewalk.

Behind the house and on either side stretched marshy land that, he'd read on the city's website, provided refuge for hundreds of bird species as well as wildlife from rabbits to coyotes. As for vegetation and terrain, the site had mentioned pickleweed, cattails, mudflats and tidal sloughs. No wonder the place stank.

Yet Geoff Humphreys's wife, Paula, a second-grade teacher, had declared the estuary far more interesting than the sailboat-filled marina that gave Safe Harbor its name, or the enticing stretch of sandy beach on the west side of town. Edmond supposed that the educator had a valid perspective, but he was far from impressed. The house itself appeared inviting, though, with a wide front porch and clean white paint trimmed in blue.

As he rang the bell, his niece pressed against his side. Dawn had become shy this past year, which was understandable in view of the turmoil in her family. With matters still unsettled, Edmond was doing his best to keep her spirits up.

The door flew open. Two girlish faces, both topped by curly red hair, peered out eagerly. "Hi!" declared the taller one, whom he guessed to be about twelve. "I'm Tiffany, Jack's niece. Well, he's our cousin really, but he's more like an uncle."

"I'm Amber," said the younger one, who wore a matching blue dress with red-and-white trim.

"Nice to meet you. I'm Edmond Everhart and this is Dawn." He saw no reason to explain further.

As they entered the house, Dawn indicated circlets of blue-and-white blossoms atop the girls' heads. "What pretty flowers!"

"We're the flower girls," Amber said. "See, we match!" She pointed to the blossoms festooning the banister of the nearby staircase.

Tiffany regarded Edmond speculatively. "Everhart. Are you related to Melissa?"

"Yes. Is she around?" He'd rather not provide details of his marital situation.

"She's in the kitchen."

"But the wedding's that way." Amber pointed to their right.

"Thank you both." Amused by the unconventional welcome, Edmond escorted Dawn into the high-ceilinged living room.

Curio cabinets dominated the far wall, with a striped sofa positioned beneath the front windows, no doubt shifted to provide space in the center. Several dozen chairs, half of them already filled, faced a slightly elevated dining room at the rear. Its table had been moved to accommodate a flower-covered arch, while a boom box in one corner played an instrumental version of "We've Only Just Begun."

Edmond recognized some of the guests as hospital staff. In his law practice, he'd learned to quickly commit names and faces to memory, and he was trying to place as many as possible when a small hand tugged his sleeve. "What's up, tiger?" he asked.

"Let's go see Aunt Lissa." Dawn peered across the room. "That girl said she was in the kitchen."

"It would be rude to barge through the house." Immediately regretting his phrasing, Edmond added, "I'm sure she'll join us later. We can talk to her then."

"I want to see her now." The girl's lower lip quivered. "I miss Aunt Lissa."

"How well do you remember her?" Dawn had been only four when they divorced. Edmond's sister Barbara had mentioned that Melissa had sent a birthday present for her daughter the following year, but Barb's life was chaotic, with many changes of both physical and email addresses. To the best of his knowledge, the two women hadn't stayed in touch.

"She used to read to me. Why did she leave?" Dawn glared up at him accusingly, as if it was his fault she'd lost one of her small circle of loved ones. Well, perhaps it was, in part.

"We divorced, but I'm sure she's missed you, too. I suppose we could take a peek." Melissa *had* emphasized the informality of the occasion.

"Yay!" Dawn gave a little hop, brown curls bouncing. Her Grandma Isabel, Edmond's stepmother, had done a fine job of styling the child's hair—not only for the wedding but also for an earlier, less pleasant outing this morning.

They were saved the need to intrude past the wedding bower when Melissa, blond hair shining above a pink dress, emerged into the dining room. Her gaze met his, then fixed on the little girl beside him.

"Dawn?" Her expression warming, Melissa descended the two steps from the elevated level. "My goodness, you've grown."

"Aunt Lissa!" The child flung herself forward. As her arms stretched to embrace her aunt, she halted in confusion. "You've grown, too."

Melissa laughed and hugged the child around her enlarged midsection. "I'm pregnant."

"You are?" Dawn patted the extended tummy. "He's a big baby."

"That's because…" She broke off suddenly.

"Is something wrong?" Edmond touched her elbow to steady her.

"No." She cleared her throat. "It's just that…"

"He's a she and she's coming in triplicate." A fortyish man with a short beard and black top hat joined the conversation from the side.

"You're having three babies?" Dawn asked.

"That's right," her aunt said. "All girls."

Triplets. Melissa didn't do things by half measures, Edmond thought. "Congratulations."

Dawn patted her aunt's tummy again. "What are their names?"

"I haven't decided."

"Can I pick?"

Melissa brushed a curl off the little girl's forehead. "I'm not ready to name them yet."

What else was one supposed to say under the circumstances? Edmond wondered."When are you due?" he asked.

"December," she said. "If I can hold out that long."

That exhausted his very short repertoire of small talk on the subject. Besides, in Edmond's opinion, this was far from a light topic, since multiple pregnancies carried extra risks. "I hope this won't endanger your health."

"She's being closely monitored." The bearded man extended his hand. "I'm the groom's uncle, Rod Vintner."

"We've met before." He shook hands with the man, who then solemnly did the same with Dawn. She giggled. "At the hospital."

"Ah, that's right." The man nodded.

"Rod's an anesthesiologist," Melissa said to Dawn. "He puts patients to sleep while they're in surgery."

"And I'll soon be sleeping myself, here at Casa Wiggins," Rod announced. "I'm trading residences with the bride. She's moving into the apartment Jack and I shared, and I'm taking her old room."

"Ah."

Don't get ideas now that you're living with my wife.

Where had that notion come from? Edmond had no claim on Melissa. Besides, a positive aspect occurred to him. "I'm glad she'll have an M.D. on hand."

"I don't deliver babies." Rod waggled his eyebrows. "Come to think of it, I don't make house calls, either."

"But you'll live here," Dawn pointed out.

"You're right," Melissa said. "He can serve as the house physician."

"Living together means we'll all be one big happy family, and doctors don't provide medical care to family members," the man deadpanned.

"You wouldn't help her?" Dawn demanded.

"Of course he would," Melissa assured the child. "Rod's joking."

"It's lucky his patients are asleep," Dawn replied tartly. "'Cause his jokes aren't funny."

Edmond laughed at the unexpected jab. The man in the top hat clutched his side. "Ow! A direct hit."

"I'm impressed," Melissa said. "You have a wicked wit, Dawn."

She took her aunt's hand. "Will you sit with us?"

"Of course."

"On that note, I have best man duties to attend to." Rod patted his pocket, which presumably held the ring, and went to join an older man in a suit waiting beneath the arch.

"That must be the minister," Edmond observed.

"He's from Karen's church." Melissa glanced toward the kitchen door. "I'm supposed to be helping her with the food."

"Isn't the ceremony about to start?" The invitation said 2 p.m., and it was almost that now. The seats had been filling as they spoke. "If we wait any longer, we'll be sitting on the window ledge."

"You're right." Melissa led the way down the narrow aisle to three empty seats. The folding chairs, fitted with white covers, weren't exactly comfortable, but Edmond found room to stretch his legs beneath the seat in front of him.

Being near Melissa was a treat. Just the musical sound of her voice calmed him. During their marriage, her nearness had filled the dark spaces in Edmond's soul. With her, he hadn't had to throw up protective walls. She'd understood him intuitively, which was why he'd expected her to understand that his vasectomy was a declaration of how strongly he felt about preserving their union.

She had a gift for nurturing, and he'd needed that. He still did. But she'd chosen motherhood over him.

Dawn, too, seemed to retain a bond with her. In the seat between them, the little girl hung on to her aunt as if she might disappear at any moment. In Dawn's world, people vanished too often. The therapist Edmond had hired for her said she suffered from separation anxiety.

"You look like a princess," Dawn told Melissa.

"So do you." She fingered the little girl's curls. "Who fixed your hair?"

"Grandma Isabel." Nodding at Melissa's bulge, she asked, "Who's the daddy?"

That brought a flush to his ex-wife's cheeks. "It's a long story."

"Can you make it shorter?"

"Sorry. Not now," Melissa said gently. "Another time."

Reluctantly, the little girl subsided. "Okay."

Edmond hoped his niece wouldn't demand that *he* explain. While he believed she was acquainted with the facts of procreation, artificial insemination seemed too intimate a subject for an uncle to describe.

"How's your mommy?" Melissa asked.

Oh, damn. Edmond wished he'd had a chance to bring up his sister's situation sooner. But before he could find the right words, Dawn blurted, "We visited Mommy in jail this morning. She's scared."

Nearby, several heads turned. "Barbara's in jail?" Melissa regarded Edmond with concern.

"I'll fill you in later." Surely she would have read the articles in the newspaper about the robbery. However, the reports had misstated Barb's last name as Greeley, although she and Simon had never married.

Melissa's nod conveyed her understanding, and she directed her next question to Dawn. "Who are you staying with?"

"Grandma and Grandpa."

"My father and stepmother, not Simon's," Edmond clarified. Simon's parents—an ex-convict father whose whereabouts were unknown and an alcoholic mother with half a dozen children by assorted men—had no contact with Dawn.

"I'm glad you brought her with you." Melissa reached across her niece to touch Edmond's hand. "And that you're here."

So was he. All the same, he couldn't resist teasing. "Glad I ignored your request?"

"Oh, Eddie, is it written somewhere that we're forbidden to get everything we want?" Her wistfulness curled inside him.

The discovery that she, too, had regrets, or at least doubts, warmed him. "I'm beginning to think so," he admitted.

He might have added more, but just then a handsome man in a dark suit joined Rod and the minister at the arch. Dawn stared, entranced. "Is that the groom? He could be a movie star."

"That's Jack," Melissa confirmed. "He's an obstetrician. The nurses at the hospital went into mourning when he got engaged to Anya."

Jack beamed with happiness. He and Anya hadn't had an easy relationship, Edmond knew, but overcoming obstacles had apparently bonded them all the more strongly.

Too bad it hadn't worked that way with us.

A muscular fellow knelt by the boom box to change the recording. Tattoos peeked from beneath his shirt collar. "Who's that?" Edmond asked.

"One of our housemates, Lucky Mendez, R.N."

Dawn studied the man dubiously. "He's a nurse?"

"Men can be nurses, too. He assists Dr. Cole Rattigan, the head of the men's fertility program," Melissa said, adding, "Also, he just earned a master's degree in nursing administration."

"What's he plan to do with that?" Edmond asked.

"Hopefully stay in Safe Harbor, if the men's fertility program expands, although that's up in the air." Melissa cast the fellow a sympathetic glance. "Otherwise he might have to find a position elsewhere."

"My daddy had tattoos," Dawn put in.

Melissa frowned. "Had, past tense?"

"He died about six months ago." Edmond didn't care to say anything more around his niece.

Dismay clouded Melissa's expression. "I've missed a lot."

"I've missed *you*," Dawn said, and smiled when her aunt kissed the top of her head.

The music changed to a march. Conversations among the guests died out.

From the front hall, the younger flower girl entered. Clutching a bouquet, she strode up the aisle a little too fast for the music.

"Slow down, for Pete's sake," growled a bulldog of a man sitting on the aisle.

The girl—Amber, Edmond recalled—flinched and

slowed. Her sister, following, scowled at the man from outside his range of vision.

Edmond raised an eyebrow questioningly at Melissa. Leaning close, she murmured, "That's the girls' stepfather. Vince Adams."

"The billionaire." A private equity investor, Vincent Adams was famous throughout Southern California for his business success and for his ruthlessness. He was also, Edmond had learned from the hospital administrator, considering donating millions of dollars to expand the men's fertility program.

As the girls took places by the arch, a pretty young woman in a dress matching theirs marched up the aisle. "That's Anya's sister Sarah," Melissa murmured. "Anya has a big family. They couldn't all come, but they're planning a reception in Colorado after the baby's born."

"How big a family?" Dawn whispered.

"She's one of seven kids."

"Wow."

The music shifted to "Here Comes the Bride." Anya entered from the hall on the arm of a distinguished older man, no doubt her father. Edmond wasn't up on the latest fashions in wedding gowns, but this one was suitably white with a lot of lace. It skimmed Anya's expanded midsection, a reminder that she was only a few months from delivering her own baby.

"Is *everybody* pregnant?" Dawn asked, a little too loudly. Nearby, several people chuckled. "I'm sorry."

Noting her tense expression, Edmond leaned close. "It's a fair question," he whispered.

"Yes, this house is baby central," Melissa said softly.

Dawn relaxed. The poor kid sometimes acted as if she carried the weight of the world, Edmond thought.

It was her parents' job to protect her childhood. Too bad they'd failed. Who would protect her now?

To MELISSA, JOY illuminated the familiar room. How Anya glowed as her father handed her to the groom. Judging by Jack's grin, it took all his self-control not to hoist Anya in his arms and whisk her off to their secret honeymoon destination, which Melissa had discovered was Santa Catalina Island. Rod had mentioned it to Karen, who'd passed it on to Melissa. Secrets didn't stay secret long in Casa Wiggins.

Located a little over twenty miles off the California coast, the island was noted for its old-fashioned charm and for ocean-related activities in its clear waters, including snorkeling and viewing undersea life from glass-bottom boats. Jack had arranged for them to stay at a romantic Victorian bed-and-breakfast with a view of the small-boat harbor in the town of Avalon.

How wonderful that the baby, whom they planned to name after both their grandmothers, would be born to such a loving pair. She was a lucky little girl.

A fluttery sensation alerted Melissa that her as-yet-nameless babies were stirring. Whenever she tried to focus on names for them, her mind went blank. Well, what was the rush?

Beneath the arch, Jack kept peeking at his bride, tuning out the minister. Anya gave him a poke, which restored him to the proper demeanor.

How comfortable they were with each other, Melissa reflected. Edmond's and her ceremony had been more formal, although every bit as enchanting. Her father, a psychologist, and her mother, a high-school math teacher, had treated her to the wedding of her dreams. A hotel ballroom in Santa Monica, the coastal city where they'd lived, had provided a fairy-tale setting for soul mates embarking on a life together. Or so she'd believed.

She'd met Edmond in a coffee shop at UCLA, where she'd been earning her master's degree in molecular biology and Edmond had been a law student. She'd admired his boldness in taking a seat at the table with her and her friends. He'd been a complete stranger but he'd teasingly claimed they kept running into each other. After she played along, they'd stayed to talk hours after her friends left. From then on, they'd gravitated to each other, a pair of intense high-achievers who shared many of the same political and social views. Their wedding day had been the happiest day of her life.

During her painful recovery from the divorce, friends had repeatedly advised her to throw her wedding album away, but Melissa couldn't imagine sacrificing those memories. There was an especially lovely photo of her with the maid of honor, Edmond's sister, Barbara, who'd bloomed with sixteen-year-old innocence.

Only a few months later, Barbara had run off to live with an ex-con. Despite Edmond's protests, his normally stern father had refused to call the police. Edmond himself had tried hard to reach out to his sister, calling and dropping by her place, but Barbara had refused to talk and Simon had threatened him.

Why hadn't her parents struggled harder to keep her? They could have brought charges against the man. As for Edmond, he'd taken his sister's rejection hard, as if he'd failed her. Melissa suspected the situation had reinforced his conviction that he wasn't cut out for parenthood. She'd soothed him as best she could, hoping that he'd heal. She'd learned the hard way that he hadn't.

Now, Dawn's mother was in jail. What crime had Barbara committed? How long would she be separated from her daughter?

While the minister expanded on the transformative power of marriage, Dawn wiggled in her seat. Edmond murmured to her—Melissa caught the words *soon* and *food*.

"Okay, Uncle Eddie." Trustingly, Dawn rested her cheek on his arm.

A glaze of tears in his eyes might not seem remarkable, considering how many people cried at weddings. But to Melissa, they showed how much Edmond's usually guarded heart was aching for this little girl. Was he finally discovering a paternal instinct?

These past three years, she'd pictured him enjoying his freedom, traveling abroad the way they used to. She'd fought painful images of him finding a woman who shared his tastes and his pleasures.

Instead, here he was, still single. Evidently he'd been tied up with family issues. He'd shouldered an unusual amount of responsibilities since his teen years, with his father frequently off driving long-distance truck routes and his reticent mother intimidated by her strong-willed daughter. Edmond's efforts to help raise his sister had smashed head-on into her adolescent rebellion. No wonder he'd craved peace and quiet as an adult.

As Anya and Jack exchanged rings and said their vows, tears blurred Melissa's own gaze. She and Edmond couldn't go back to their wedding day eight years ago and make things come out differently. Yet today he was showing a different side of himself....

What an idiot she was! When she entered into this pregnancy, she'd been well aware that she couldn't expect any man to love and care for her *and* her babies. Her longing for them had overwhelmed all other considerations.

They were enough to fill up her life and her heart. They had to be.

Chapter Four

Edmond had intended to stay after the ceremony only long enough to be polite. He'd assumed his presence might be uncomfortable for Melissa.

Instead, she was friendly toward him, while Dawn eagerly joined the red-haired flower girls at the buffet table in an area connecting the kitchen and den. He was glad he'd brought her. His niece could use a change of scenery to take her mind off visiting her mom in jail.

Worse might lie ahead for Barbara. Edmond tried not to dwell on that disturbing prospect. He needed today's change of pace as much as Dawn.

"You and your housemates are wonderful cooks," he told Melissa as they waited in line. Delicious smells wafted from the array of dishes, while a separate table displayed a three-tiered white cake decked with blue and red berries and, on top, a large red heart. Plates of cookies surrounded it, presumably for those too impatient to wait for dessert.

"The food is mostly Karen's doing. I'm the baker. I can't take credit for the wedding cake, though," she added. "I'm the cookie lady."

"I'm impressed by anything people do in a kitchen, other than set fires." Growing up, Edmond had learned the basics, but rarely cooked.

"When we moved into the house, the five of us voted to take turns, each fixing dinner for a week. That didn't last," Melissa admitted. "Now we all pitch in or go our own ways."

"The kitchen must have been upgraded." From where they stood, Edmond noted gleaming new appliances.

"Karen remodeled after her mother died last year," Melissa said. "She didn't change the basic shape of the room, though. You still have to perform the limbo to get into the pantry."

"So she inherited the place. I was wondering why she bought a house here, considering the smell. Although the scenery *is* striking." Sliding glass doors offered a view across the patio and rear yard to the gray-and-green estuary. "What's the layout—any bedrooms downstairs?" While he didn't expect a tour of the place, Edmond was curious about the sleeping arrangements.

"Lucky has a small suite through there." She indicated a doorway on the far side of the den. "Karen, Zora, Anya and I have bedrooms upstairs."

"Except now Rod's taking Anya's place," he muttered, half to himself.

Melissa ducked her head. "I keep forgetting."

"Won't that be awkward, having a guy upstairs with the ladies?"

In a low tone, she confided, "He and Karen have become close. I hope that won't blow up in our faces, but she seems happy, and he's a solid guy underneath the kidding."

"Yes, I got that impression."

As Edmond filled his plate at the serving table, he recalled his intention of cultivating new acquaintances. There were a lot of people here, and he supposed he could chat them up, but he'd much rather spend the afternoon in Melissa's company.

Also, he suspected many of the guests, aside from those he'd already met, were from out-of-town. The father of the bride was busy tending to his wife, who moved stiffly with the aid of a cane. Jack was introducing his friends to a fiftyish woman dressed in knock-your-eyes-out Caribbean colors. Edmond had heard that Jack's mother lived in Haiti and raised money for charities there.

He decided to forget duty for one day. Aside from keeping an eye on Dawn, of course. She and the two older girls had gone outside to eat at the patio table. Before they closed the glass door behind them, Dawn had sent Edmond a questioning gaze. He nodded his approval. If the girls didn't mind the smell, more power to them.

"I'm glad she's found playmates," he said, following Melissa to a well-worn couch. "She tends to be shy, especially with new people. Jack's nieces seem outgoing."

"Except around their stepfather," she murmured.

Edmond didn't spot Vince Adams or his wife in the den, although they'd been at the head of the buffet line. He assumed the couple had carried their plates into the dining room, where some of Melissa's housemates had put back the dining room table and set it immediately after the ceremony. That suited him fine. No matter how important the Adamses might be as potential donors, Edmond was in no mood for apple-polishing, especially to a guy who'd publicly humiliated his stepdaughter.

"You're good with Dawn." Melissa set her plate on the coffee table.

"I try." He stared moodily at his food. "Let's hope I do better with her than I did with my sister. I wish I understood where I went wrong."

"Why do you blame yourself for her problems?" she asked.

"When we were young and Dad was on the road, Barbara used to confide in me about everything, value my advice, follow me around. But when she hit adolescence, I was commuting to college so I couldn't be there for her.

She began acting out, cutting school, skipping her home-work assignments."

"Many teenagers rebel to a degree," she pointed out.

"Sure, but then she ran off with Simon. I should have done more to stop her." It had been only a few months after their marriage. "She was sixteen. We could have gone to the police."

"That was your parents' decision, not yours," she re-minded him. "And she did get legally emancipated after Dawn's birth."

"I can't shake the sense that I let her down. Did she men-tion why she'd been so eager to leave home?" While Ed-mond knew Simon could be charming and manipulative, surely his sister hadn't been totally blind to the man's faults.

"I sensed she was angry, but not necessarily at you. She didn't say anything specific, though." Flecks of green stood out in Melissa's hazel eyes. "I tried to talk to her after she had the baby, about planning a future for herself and Dawn, but she pushed me away. Edmond, why is she in jail? That sounds serious."

"It is." Months of holding his emotions in check, of standing strong for everyone around him, yielded to the relief of confiding in a person he trusted. "That jerk Simon talked her into driving the getaway car for a robbery."

"I can't believe she'd do something that stupid." Melissa set down her fork, giving him her full attention.

Around them, people mingled and chatted. Edmond saw Karen glance their way as if about to approach, but he shook his head. She went in another direction. He decided he liked that woman. "According to Barbara—after the fact—Simon claimed he owed money to a criminal gang and that if he didn't pay up, they'd kill him."

"Was it true?"

"I have no idea." Either way, that didn't excuse the man's crimes, nor Barb's. "During the robbery, he and a policeman traded gunfire, and Simon was fatally wounded. The officer escaped injury, mercifully."

That was fortunate both for the officer and for Barbara. Under California law, the district attorney could have charged her with murder just for being a participant in the robbery. However, perhaps doubting that a jury would convict her of murder under the circumstances, the D.A. had only charged her with robbery.

"Your sister was waiting in the getaway car?" Melissa asked.

"That's right." She hadn't witnessed the shooting, but she'd heard gunfire. "Simon staggered into the passenger seat. While she was arguing that they should go to a hospital, he died."

Melissa shook her head. "How awful."

"I can't spare any regrets for that man," Edmond said bitterly. "He ruined my sister's life—with her compliance."

"What about Dawn? Where was she during all this?"

"She'd gone to the beach with a friend's family." The shootout had occurred on a Saturday, while his niece was out of school. "The police contacted my father and stepmother, who called me. I picked her up and broke the news." He clenched his fists at the memory.

Edmond had built up to the subject gradually during the drive from the beach, telling his niece as much as he'd learned of the robbery and assuring her that her mother was unharmed but under arrest. Dawn had taken the news of Simon's death solemnly, her response hard to read.

Then, tearfully, she'd asked, "Is it because I was mad at him?"

Shocked, Edmond had assured her that Simon's death wasn't her fault. "Neither you nor I nor anyone else has magical powers," he'd told her, hoping that was the right thing to say. "This has nothing to do with you. Why were you mad at him?"

"He yelled at me for leaving my toys out."

Edmond hadn't been sure a seven-year-old understood what death meant, but later, after he'd hired a therapist, she'd insisted that Dawn did understand. Grieving was a complex process, she'd added. As Dawn entered new phases of development, she'd revisit the loss. For now, she needed to feel secure that the other people she loved weren't going to disappear from her world, too.

Unfortunately, Edmond couldn't promise that about Barbara. He could only do his best to hold Dawn's world together. Given his poor track record with his sister, he sometimes panicked over the missteps he might make.

Melissa touched his arm, a soothing gesture that brought him back to this comfortable room and cheerful gathering. "Dawn's been through a lot this past year," she said. "So have you and Barbara."

"It's been rough." He sketched the rest of the sorry tale. After Barb's arrest, a judge had granted bail, and she and Dawn had moved in with his father, Mort, and stepmother, Isabel, a retired nurse's aide. During the trial, the grandparents had helped supervise the little girl, with frequent visits from Edmond until the jury had come back with the verdict two weeks ago. The jurors had convicted his sister of robbery and related charges. "Her sentencing is Monday afternoon."

She blinked. "The day after tomorrow?"

"That's right." Edmond had already arranged to take the day off work to be there for moral support. Barb's defense attorney, Joseph Noriega, had submitted a sentencing memorandum requesting leniency. By now the judge also had a probation report and the prosecutor's recommendation. Edmond suspected they'd be less favorable.

Melissa's hand cupped his. "What kind of sentence is she facing?"

"Minimum, a year in county jail plus probation."

"And the maximum?"

Noriega had warned them to prepare for a longer term, to be served in state prison. "I'm trying not to dwell on it. Let's wait till we know for sure."

"How can the judge separate her from her little girl any longer than necessary?" Melissa asked.

"She's the one who chose to break the law." As an attorney, Edmond was a sworn officer of the court, and he understood the legal perspective. "If Simon had lived, she might have negotiated a deal based on testifying against him. But that's not possible now."

The prosecutor had had no difficulty winning a conviction. The jury had reached a verdict in three hours, which was lightning speed, considering that they'd also had to elect a foreman, fill out paperwork and review multiple counts during that time.

Melissa returned to her main concern. "You said she'll be in jail at least a year. What are the arrangements for Dawn?"

"That reminds me, I'd better check on her. I'll tell you in a minute." Before he could rise, however, Edmond observed his niece entering with the other girls, then sliding the glass door shut behind them. Tiffany shepherded the little band into the kitchen with their empty plates and glasses.

While the youngsters were out of earshot, he said, "My Dad and Isabel indicated they'd take her, with my assistance. But that's not settled."

"What do you mean?" Worry suffused Melissa's expressive face. She'd always been empathetic, and he recalled how she used to love holding Dawn on her lap and paging through picture books with the little girl.

Had that been a factor in her change of heart about having children? Later, he'd tried to figure out how she could have changed her opinions so dramatically without his awareness, and perhaps her relationship with Dawn had been a clue. But it wasn't enough to explain her sudden shift.

How ironic that he was now forced to step in as a substitute parent of sorts. "While Barb was preparing for trial, she was afraid that if she were convicted, the authorities might put Dawn in foster care," he answered.

"That would be horrible!"

"Yes." It didn't take an expert in child psychology to understand how traumatic that would be for everyone. "Barb wanted to assign temporary guardianship to Isabel and Dad, but they were too tied up with Dad's medical issues to go to family court with her."

"Medical issues?"

"Skin cancer." He explained briefly that his father had undergone treatment and tests now showed him to be cancer-free. Then he continued, "Appointment of a guardian requires a judge's approval." Nearly hysterical with fear for her daughter's well-being as the trial date approached, Barbara had begged Edmond to take emergency guardianship himself.

"What did you do?" Melissa watched him intently.

"I agreed, even though I'm obviously not the ideal person to raise a little girl." That was an understatement for a guy who lacked paternal instincts, had failed miserably in protecting his sister, and lived in a one-bedroom apartment.

However, he refused to abandon his family. He'd promised in court to take responsibility for Dawn, and he meant it. If necessary, he'd move in with his parents for a year and commute an hour each way from their home in Norwalk, in eastern Los Angeles County. It would be uncomfortable and inconvenient, but he'd do it for Dawn and for Barbara.

"Dawn said she was staying with your parents," Melissa reminded him.

"She and Barb were already living there." He blew out

a long breath. "We all agreed it's vital that she have what her therapist calls 'continuity of care.'"

"I'm glad she has a counselor," Melissa said. "That doesn't substitute for being with her mom, though. Why couldn't Barb stay out on bail until she's sentenced?"

"She's considered a flight risk." The Mexican border was only a couple of hours' drive away.

"That's too bad." Melissa regarded him with a warmth he'd missed—a lot. "Edmond, what you're doing for Dawn, protecting her so she won't go into foster care, it's wonderful."

"I would never let her be yanked away from her family." To him, it was the only decent way to behave. He'd been blessed with many gifts, including loving if flawed parents, educational opportunities and an aptitude for the law. Surely there was a reason he'd also been given enough strength to stand tall when others needed him. Though it was a relief to express the situation openly to someone, without fear of judgment.

He'd done his best to be there for Melissa after her parents' deaths. And he'd counted on her being there for him, too.

"Did it occur to you that you might have paternal instincts after all?" she asked.

"I'm sorry?"

"You have a big heart," she said gently. "Big enough to love more than one person. You'd make a wonderful father."

He stiffened. Just when he'd believed she understood him, she was viewing his confidence through the lens of her own wishes, trying to convert him into her idea of what a man ought to be. "I'm not her father, I'm her guardian."

"I've seen how you act with her," Melissa said. "You've changed these past three years."

Not that much.

This past year had been one blow after another. Edmond

had rarely had a chance to replenish his inner strength with quiet hours to read, visit museums and travel. The worst part had been enduring these crises alone. That was, in part, why he'd opened up to Melissa today. To his disappointment, her attitude reminded him that she didn't accept him for himself, only as a wish-fulfillment fantasy.

It was important to clear up that misunderstanding. "Don't interpret my actions to suit your assumptions. My views on fatherhood haven't changed."

"Are you sure you have an accurate perception of yourself?"

How insulting. "While I respect your decision to have children in whatever manner you choose, you shouldn't cast me in the role of father-knows-best simply because it's convenient."

Her mouth tightened. "That's not what I was doing."

Instinctively, he echoed her earlier words. "Are you sure *you* have an accurate perception of yourself?"

"Don't be arrogant!" As she leaned forward to pick up her plate, a startled expression crossed her face and her hand flew to her midsection.

"Is anything wrong?" Although she didn't appear distressed, Edmond hadn't forgotten the bout of nausea in her office.

Melissa shook her head, blond tendrils quivering. "They're scooting around in there."

"You can feel the babies?" She'd mentioned being due in December, he recalled, and that was many months off. "How big are they?"

"Four or five inches apiece." A smile bloomed, and wonder touched Melissa's eyes. "They're small, but I can tell when they're active."

While the gestation and birth process *was* miraculous, Edmond couldn't pretend to share her enthusiasm. "Doesn't it feel strange, having other people living inside you?"

She chuckled. "What a funny way to put it. This is normal."

"Having triplets?"

"Not that part."

Across the room, someone clapped for the guests' attention. At the cake table, Zora Raditch, one of Melissa's housemates, waved a metal spatula. "We're doing the cut-the-cake thing now, and if either bride or groom shoves a slice in the other person's face, I will personally smash the entire remaining cake over that person's head. Fair warning!"

A ripple of laughter greeted this announcement. Edmond, however, was concerned about the baby bump visible beneath the woman's dress. Another unmarried pregnancy in the house wouldn't concern him, but he'd represented Zora in her divorce from a self-centered businessman named Andrew. Despite an agreement to negotiate fairly, the man had played games with the settlement and with signing the papers.

That had all been resolved, finally. But what about this pregnancy? "Dare I ask if Andrew's the father?" In Edmond's opinion, a child deserved better than to be born into such a mixed-up situation.

"Yes, he is, sad to say." Melissa arose gracefully considering her awkward distribution of weight. "They had break-up sex. Then he went and married his new girlfriend."

Edmond collected their plates. "He has obligations, regardless. Their child is legally entitled to parental support."

"It's children, plural. Twins." Melissa shrugged. "I'm not sure why, but I don't believe Zora's even broken the news to Andrew. She can't keep her pregnancy secret from him long, since her former mother-in-law works at the hospital."

"Please let her know I'd be happy to help." Regardless of Andrew's attitudes toward fatherhood, he had obligations to these children. And he owed his former wife his support during her pregnancy, as well. "She shouldn't have to go through this alone."

"She isn't alone," Melissa reminded him. "She has me and Karen."

"Five babies. I'd call that a full house."

"Plus Anya's having a baby. But that little girl's father gives a damn." With that, Melissa went to join the gathering around the cake table.

I'm not the father of your babies. Her unjustified anger annoyed Edmond. Well, he *was* responsible for his niece, and no one could accuse him of not giving a damn about her.

On Monday, he'd find out exactly how big a responsibility he'd undertaken. Hopefully, this would prove to be an unpleasant but limited blip in his sister's troubled life, and Dawn could resume living with her. Pushing aside his worries, Edmond carried the dirty dishes to the kitchen.

Chapter Five

The savory scent hit Melissa's senses the moment she opened the oven door. Orange and lemon zest, balsamic vinegar, olive oil and a touch of sweetness—it transported her instantly to a cozy hotel in Sorrento she and Edmond had used as a base for exploring southern Italy during one of their favorite trips.

She'd discovered this unusual muffin recipe on a website. After her roommates tasted it, the muffins had become an instant hit.

With the aroma, perhaps because she'd encountered her ex-husband yesterday, memories flooded in. As she set the hot tin on the stovetop and began transferring the muffins to a wire cooling rack, Melissa recalled the view from their hilltop hotel over the deep blue Gulf of Naples.

She and Edmond had spent days exploring the partially restored ruins of Pompeii and Herculaneum, which had been buried in the eruption of Mount Vesuvius in 79 A.D. Images of her husband remained etched in her memory: sweat darkening his shirt as he led the way along a narrow, ancient street; his grin shining from his sun-darkened face as they shared a glass of red wine over lunch; his boyish enthusiasm for the voluptuous frescoes decorating two-thousand-year-old palatial homes. They'd hated to leave Sorrento, even though they were continuing on to Rome, Florence and Venice.

If only she could live two lives, Melissa reflected wistfully as she fetched a box of powdered sugar from the cupboard. In the other life, she and Edmond would continue to travel together and, when at home, spend cozy Sunday mornings nestled on the couch, sharing the newspaper. There'd be no risk of provoking his rejection, because she wouldn't long for babies.

But she would never give up this reality. Inside her, as if to reassert their presence, the little ones squirmed. Melissa smiled, imagining her daughters' rambunctious play. She'd read that multiples interacted in the womb. Was one of them already bossy? Was another learning to assert herself in response?

"Ooh, Italian muffins!" Zora bounced into the kitchen, although how anyone five months pregnant with twins could bounce was beyond Melissa. Her housemate's hand shot toward the cooling rack.

"Stop!" Melissa cried. "They'll burn you. Besides, they aren't powdered yet."

"Can I help?" Without waiting, Zora plucked the box from her hands. Since Melissa had pried the spout partway open, soft sugar floated out, touching Zora's ginger-colored hair with white and speckling the floor. "Oh, sorry. I'll clean up."

"No, you won't." Melissa removed the sugar from her grasp before any more escaped. "Neither you nor I ought to be kneeling on the floor."

"We aren't invalids." Zora rarely requested assistance or complained about her pregnancy-related ills, except perhaps to Anya. The two had shared an apartment before moving into this house, and initially their pregnancies had drawn them closer. But Anya was on her honeymoon now, and had already packed most of her possessions to move in with Jack.

"We may not be invalids but we should be sensible," Melissa told her.

"Don't lecture me. I get more than enough of that already." Zora flinched as a heavy tread crossing the den announced Lucky's approach. "Speak of the devil."

"Behave," Melissa cautioned her friend. "He's a prince of a guy."

"You mean a royal pain?"

Melissa chuckled. "Lucky can be that, too."

"Do I hear someone taking my name in vain?" The male nurse appeared in the doorway, his dark eyes sweeping to Zora. Melissa wondered if either of them noticed how he always focused on her first, no matter who else was around.

Although Lucky wasn't Melissa's type, she appreciated his macho appeal, from his cropped hair to his colorful tattoos of a dragon and a sword-wielding woman in skimpy armor. These were revealed today, along with his sculpted muscles, by a sleeveless black T-shirt. New acquaintances often reacted with surprise on learning he was a nurse and a vegetarian, as if those aspects were incompatible with rough-hewn virility.

"No more than usual," Zora said.

"I'm not sure how to interpret that, so I'll ignore it."

Melissa was glad Lucky didn't respond with a jab. He and Zora could pick at each other no end, and Sunday mornings ought to be restful.

When he moved into the kitchen, Melissa halted him with an upraised hand. "Don't step there." She pointed to the spilled sugar. "If you would please clean that up, I'll finish sifting this on the muffins."

"Sure thing. Since you're baking, it's the least I can do." Cheerfully, Lucky went to fetch cleaning supplies. He really was a good housemate.

"I'll brew coffee." Zora took out the canister, although neither she nor Melissa had a taste for it these days. Still,

Karen would be down soon, and she didn't function well till she'd had her first cup.

"I should have put some on earlier," Melissa reflected.

"Why should you? I just want to look busy. And thanks for not telling him I spilled it," Zora said in a low voice. "He expects everyone to be perfect."

"Not everyone. Just you." For some reason, Lucky was harder on Zora than on anyone else.

Zora measured the coffee, careful to avoid any further spillage. "It's none of his business whether I inform Andrew about the babies. If I go after my ex for support, he'll jerk me around, maybe sue for custody just so he feels like he's on top. He always has to win."

"What about Betsy?" Andrew's mother, Betsy Raditch, was the hospital's director of nursing. Since Zora worked as an ultrasound tech, she wasn't directly under Betsy's supervision, but they'd remained on friendly terms after Zora had split with Andrew. "She must have noticed."

"She hasn't asked who the father is, and I haven't told her. No sense putting her in the middle." Zora broke off as Lucky returned. He wiped the floor without comment.

Melissa finished sugaring the muffins and put them on a platter. After setting one aside for herself and giving Zora another, she set the plate on the table.

"May I eat now, Mommy?" Lucky joked. "I did my chores."

"Good boy," Melissa said. "Dig in."

Soon the three of them were lounging around the table with the newspaper, silent except for the occasional chuckle at a comic strip or wry comment about a news story. Melissa was grateful for the company. Before moving into the house last spring, she'd lived alone in an efficiency apartment, missing married life and yearning for a baby.

She wished she could have found the right man. But her desire for motherhood had become too powerful to resist, and being surrounded by friends provided all the support she could ask for. Most of the time, anyway.

Zora departed first. Waiting until they heard the shower running upstairs, Lucky caught Melissa's eye and said, "Since you're on positive terms with your ex, you should talk to him about Zora. As her divorce attorney, he's the best person to explain about Andrew's legal obligations."

"Zora's well aware that he owes her support," Melissa answered. "She has her reasons for keeping mum. And it isn't my business to intervene with her attorney."

"Well, she does a rotten job of taking care of herself. Her mom and stepfather live out of state, and we're the only family she has around here." Lucky set aside the sports section. "She ought to put her life in order before the twins are born."

"You think involving Andrew will put things in order?" Although Melissa didn't disagree with Lucky's premise, she also understood Zora's side. "It's a messy situation no matter what she does."

"She must love messy situations, because she's always in one." Morning light through the glass door played across his smooth olive skin. "First she had an affair with Andrew while he was married to his first wife, then, after he cheated on her, too...well, what kind of bonehead has break-up sex with a guy like that?"

"She doesn't always show the best judgment." Melissa left it at that. She didn't want to run down her friend.

"That's putting it mildly," Lucky grumbled. "Someone has to keep after her."

"Be careful about imposing your values." Melissa didn't understand why he insisted on stirring things up, unless it was a desire for control. "It's been said that you expect people to be perfect."

"I expect people to learn from their mistakes, that's all." Through the kitchen doorway, she glimpsed Karen beelining for the coffee. Her voice drifted out. "Is he on Zora's case again?"

"If there's one thing I've learned, it's that I can't win against a houseful of women." Lucky arose with the comics section and his coffee. "I'll be in my room."

"Enjoy." Since he had the downstairs suite, with a private bath and a small enclosed sunroom, Melissa had no compunctions about chasing him away.

Karen strolled in, mug in hand. She wore a crisp lavender blouse over a long gray skirt, and had coiled her thick auburn hair atop her head. "Ah, you're dressed. I was going to offer you the use of my tub." She occupied the master suite, which had a private bath.

"Thanks, but I woke early." Melissa had showered and thrown on jeans and a short-sleeved cotton sweater. "Figured I'd finish in the bathroom before Zora got up."

"These are my favorite." Karen transferred a muffin to her plate. "Listen, I know it'll be tricky once Rod moves in, sharing a bathroom and all. You can use mine whenever there's a crunch."

"Will do."

"He's coming over this morning." Karen's grin made her appear younger than her forty-two years. "We're switching Rod's stuff with Anya's as a welcome-home present for the honeymooners."

"You're putting her stuff in Jack's apartment while she's out of town?" Melissa wasn't sure she would appreciate someone else handling her property without permission. Still, it would save Anya and Jack the trouble.

"Anya's already packed the personal items," Karen pointed out. "And Rod gets lonely, rattling around in that apartment by himself."

"He's here for dinner nearly every night."

"You don't mind, do you?"

While Melissa wasn't crazy about adjusting to another

man on the premises, she enjoyed Rod's sense of humor, and as Edmond had noted, having a physician down the hall might be valuable. "He's excellent company. Jack claims his uncle can't cook worth a darn, though. Are you sure the main attraction for him isn't the meals?"

Karen laughed. "Partly, no doubt. But he helps pay for the food and does the dishes without being nagged."

"What more could one ask for?"

"Precisely."

When her friend picked up the entertainment section, Melissa resumed reading the newspaper. A few pages later, a headline leaped out at her: "Driver to Be Sentenced in Street Fair Robbery." An unflattering photo showed Barbara Everhart, her hair pulled back and her expression grim.

Most of the details in the article were familiar, but Edmond hadn't mentioned that the setting had been a street fair or that there'd been three robbery victims, all vendors. Simon Greeley, the alleged robber, had traded gunfire with a police officer and suffered fatal wounds. No one else was hit, almost a miracle in such a crowded venue.

How did a sweet sixteen-year-old girl get mixed up with that awful man?

Of course, Barb wasn't sixteen anymore. The article listed her age as twenty-four; in the photo, she looked older. There was no mention of her daughter.

Melissa lowered the paper. How strange that Edmond, the last man on earth to become a father, had accepted guardianship of his niece. Was it mostly from a sense of duty, or had he truly bonded with the child?

Meeting Dawn again yesterday had reminded Melissa that, in her heart, she was still the little girl's aunt. Divorces might divide a couple, but they didn't necessarily sever emotional connections to other family members.

The doorbell rang. "That'll be Rod." Karen rose and cut through the den.

Melissa glanced at the muffin platter. Four remained. She doubted they'd last long with Rod on the premises, not that she'd planned to save any.

From the front, she heard Rod's light tenor voice say, "Guess who I found casing the joint."

"Just remedying a mistake," came a deeper male response. "I forgot to send a wedding present, so I'm dropping this off."

Melissa's pulse sped up. She hadn't expected to run into Edmond again so soon. Swallowing, she chided herself for overreacting.

Yesterday, they'd sniped at each other. She regretted her testy remark about uncaring fathers, since her situation had nothing to do with Edmond. But his crack about not knowing herself had hit painfully close to home. Much as she treasured the triplets, she'd never expected to raise three babies by herself.

She realized now that what she'd longed for was a family with kids *and* a husband to love and care for. But she'd fallen for the wrong man, and then she'd chosen a path that led away from him. If only she'd known her own mind sooner…

Then what? *Sometimes you don't know your own mind now.* Or, as she'd concluded before, perhaps she simply couldn't have everything.

The quiet den filled with people as Lucky emerged from his lair. Amid the exchange of greetings, Melissa caught Edmond's gaze.

She managed a simple, "Hi."

With a nod, he set down a wrapped box bearing the logo of Kitchens, Cooks and Linens, the store where Anya had her bridal registry. "Those muffins smell fantastic. They remind me of Italy."

"Me, too," she said.

"I'm amazed you can smell anything after that whiff

out front." Rod, wearing a deerstalker hat worthy of Sherlock Holmes, grimaced. "I may have to have my olfactory nerves removed."

"I've smelled worse," Lucky said.

"Really? Where?" Rod demanded.

"Accident scenes. I used to drive an ambulance."

Melissa didn't hear the rest of their conversation. She was too busy trying to remain relaxed as Edmond approached. "You could have mailed the gift," she observed.

The light reflected on his glasses, obscuring his eyes. "I had an ulterior motive," he said. "To apologize for being so rough on you yesterday."

"It's fine."

"You sure?"

"I pushed you," she conceded. *Now let's change the subject.* "It was good to see Dawn."

He shifted closer. "Being around you meant more to her than I expected."

"She means a lot to me, too," she replied honestly.

Rod brushed past them to snare a muffin. "Great! An energy boost."

Edmond took one, also. After the first taste, he released an appreciative sigh. "These are just like the muffins in Sorrento."

"Close." Melissa still believed her version lacked something—perhaps the taste of the local water.

"Sorrento. Is that in Mexico?" Impossible to tell if Rod was kidding. "So, Ed, you're helping us move the bride's stuff, right?"

"Uh…"

"Right this way."

As Rod shepherded Edmond to the stairs, Melissa released her grip on the newspaper and smoothed the crumpled page.

When Edmond tasted the muffins, he'd remembered one of their happiest times together, just as she had. *If only...*

If only they could travel and simply be a couple? But she couldn't lead that alternate life of her imaginings. Wisps of memory were no substitute for planning a future together.

And there was no way they could have a future.

IT SERVED HIM right to be drafted into hard labor, Edmond reflected as he backed down the stairs, supporting one end of Anya's desk. He'd had no business intruding on Melissa's Sunday.

Embarrassed at forgetting to bring a gift to the wedding, he truly had meant to drop it off and leave. But the scent and taste of those muffins had given him pause. Melissa's choice of recipe indicated that she, too, cherished the memory of their trip. That didn't necessarily imply she cherished *him, though*—the barrier between them loomed larger than ever, literally. So why couldn't he stay away?

After the divorce, Edmond had tried dating others. None of them had measured up, and this year he'd been absorbed in his family's troubles. Now he wondered if that was the only thing preventing him from finding a new relationship.

He and Lucky eased the desk down the front porch steps. The estuary smell didn't bother Edmond as much today. He supposed one could get used to it.

"Interesting how Rod left the heavy lifting to us," Lucky observed as they carted the desk toward a rental van in the gravel parking area.

"Is that typical of him?"

"I wouldn't exactly call him lazy." Lucky's amused tone indicated that he liked his new housemate. "But he does have a knack for arranging matters to suit his convenience."

"I'm surprised an anesthesiologist hasn't bought his own house by now." Edmond would love to do that, but he'd only recently paid off his educational loans.

"He spent all his money fighting for custody of his daughters, the two little flower girls at the wedding." Lucky led the way in maneuvering the desk up the ramp. "And lost to Portia and Vince Adams."

"As their father, Rod has rights." Edmond hefted his end of the desk.

"He found out six years ago during the divorce that Portia had cheated on him and the girls weren't genetically his, even though he'd raised them as his own." Lucky shook his head. "They aren't Vince's, either, but he's rich enough to afford the best representation, if you consider scummy bottom-feeders the best. Sorry, I don't mean to speak ill of lawyers. Well, maybe I do, but I'm sure you're an exception."

"I hope so." Edmond had heard his share of lawyer jokes, along the lines of *Why don't sharks bite attorneys? Professional courtesy.* He chose not to take the cracks personally.

As for Rod, under California law, he was the children's father regardless of genetics, since he'd been married to their mother when they were born. However, a guy as rich and reputedly unscrupulous as Vince could grind an opponent into the dust with one courtroom tactic after another.

"I try to avoid contentious cases," he said. "My preference is for both sides to reach a compromise."

"Are people really willing to do that where children and divorces are concerned?"

"Not always." Edmond understood Lucky's skepticism. "But if they can move past their initial insistence on winning, most prefer to do what's in the best interests of the child. They can also save themselves money and stress."

With the desk stowed, he brushed off his hands and descended the ramp. On the driveway, Lucky stretched. "Let's hope Melissa won't be requiring your services."

What a strange remark. "Which services?"

The other man laughed. "As an attorney."

"Why would she?"

"The embryos."

Usually, Edmond was quick to grasp people's meanings, but not in this case. "She said there's no father involved. Since I assume the sperm donor signed a release, I don't understand why she'd require legal counsel."

"You haven't heard the story?" Lifting a hand, Lucky shaded his eyes against the midday glare. "She didn't use a sperm donor."

Surely Melissa hadn't been rash enough to involve a man simply on the promise that he'd stay out of the picture. "Who's the father, then?"

"The father *and* the mother are clients who donated their unused embryos." Lucky glanced toward the house. "I'm sure they signed off on the whole thing, but people can be unpredictable."

"The babies aren't hers?" That was an inaccurate assessment, Edmond realized as soon as he said it. "Genetically, I mean."

"You got it."

She was carrying babies that weren't related to her. Edmond assumed she felt a strong attachment, yet many women served as surrogates and willingly relinquished the infants. Not that he expected Melissa to do any such thing.

The more he learned, the less he understood her. When he'd moved to Safe Harbor, he'd hoped he might finally grasp what had gone wrong between them and possibly how to fix it. Instead, the picture kept getting muddier.

Yet hadn't he cherished their differences during their marriage? She'd been his refuge when he felt overwhelmed, and he'd been her strength when her world had fallen apart after her parents' deaths.

When she'd brought up the idea of becoming parents, he wished now that he'd listened to her rather than reacting the way he had. But ultimately, they'd still have stood on opposite sides of a great divide.

The front door opened. Karen emerged, toting a couple of suitcases. Behind her, Rod hefted a box, grimacing as if about to collapse beneath its weight. Either it contained heavy books or he was milking the situation.

Preoccupied by what Lucky had revealed about the embryos, Edmond was in no mood to stick around for polite chitchat, with them *or* with Melissa. After a brief farewell, he went to his car.

As for the triplets, Melissa ought to be safe from a legal perspective. And surely she loved these children. Still, these babies were the blood kin of another couple, a mom and a dad. They'd presumably borne other children, so what *were* the implications for Melissa of raising triplets who had full siblings living nearby?

Embryo donation wasn't as regulated as adoption or surrogacy. In many respects, the legal status of embryos remained unsettled, but their transfer was governed by contract law as if they were property.

This discovery changed nothing between him and Melissa. So why did he feel sucker-punched?

Chapter Six

"You can't be serious!" On the examining table, Melissa tugged the ridiculously small hospital gown around her protruding abdomen. It still failed to close. "I thought I was doing well."

"You are." Dr. Zack Sargent appeared surprised by her outburst. "I didn't say you have to go on bed rest right now. But in a couple more weeks, we should consider it."

With an effort, Melissa curbed her irritation. Her obstetrician cared about her. Zack had worked her into his Monday schedule to give her an extra checkup due to the increased risks of her pregnancy.

"My only symptoms are dry skin and trouble getting comfortable in bed," she reminded him in a calmer tone. "You said I'm in great shape for eighteen weeks."

"That's true." Zack regarded his computer terminal. An earnest man in his mid-thirties, he was the driving force behind the hospital's grant program for financially strapped clients. He was also married to Melissa's boss, Jan. "Blood pressure, weight gain, glucose levels, babies' heartbeats—everything's normal. Impressive, actually. But keeping you all healthy until delivery will be a balancing act."

"Surely lying around for months can cause problems, too." The prospect dismayed Melissa. She had too many responsibilities at work.

"Lack of activity can raise the risk of blood clots and

decrease bone mass, which is why I don't recommend complete bed rest unless absolutely necessary," he said. "However, bed rest can mean simply staying home and doing less than usual. I'm also concerned about you operating a car as you get bigger."

"Karen offered to give me a ride to and from work whenever I'm ready to stop driving." Melissa was grateful for her generous friend. "And my housemates said they'd pick up groceries for me. I don't need them to do any of that yet, but I'll accept it as soon as I do."

"Good," Zack said. "Pay attention to what your body's telling you."

"It's telling me that staying home would drive me crazy." Aware of how much he cared about the fertility program, she noted, "And it's not as if Jan can throw a temp into my position."

From the doctor's expression, she saw that her point had registered. "Talk to her about working remotely," he advised. "There's no reason you can't keep up with your email and meet with clients from home."

"I can come into the office as long as I feel okay, though, right?" Melissa pressed. "I'll put my feet up. And it should be easier for you to monitor me here at the hospital than at home."

Zack typed a note into the computer. "All true. But don't forget, there's a sixty percent chance that multiple babies will be born prematurely, plus your entire body is under stress. It's working hard even when you're resting."

Melissa closed her eyes, willing herself to relax. "I know that pregnancy is temporary and well worth the trouble. That doesn't make this easy."

"Of course not."

If she were married, things would be different, she reflected. Despite the assurances of her friends, the hospital's paid maternity leave and the staff day-care center, she experienced moments of panic about how she would cope with three babies.

If only Edmond… But that was ridiculous. He had problems of his own, and his attitude toward fatherhood hadn't changed. Also, his departure yesterday without saying goodbye puzzled her.

"Continue eating well and exercising mildly, as you've been doing," Zack concluded.

"I will." Melissa enjoyed the gentle stretching exercises she performed every morning.

"Any questions?"

She shook her head.

"I have one." He smiled. "Have you chosen their names?"

"People keep asking me that, but no." She wasn't ready. Besides, the only names in Melissa's mind today were Dawn and Barbara, whose sentencing was scheduled for this afternoon.

"Something wrong?" Zack asked.

"Nothing we haven't covered." It wasn't her place to discuss Edmond's family problems.

He assisted her off the table. "Let's schedule you for another appointment in a week. Sooner if you experience problems."

"You bet." Regretting her earlier sharpness with him, Melissa added, "I appreciate your working me in this way."

"Glad to do it."

As she dressed, she was glad she wouldn't have to face house confinement just yet, especially when she wanted to be there for her niece. Well, with luck she had a few weeks to spare. And perhaps the sentencing would't be as bad as she feared.

SITTING IN A row of tiered seats at the back of a room in Orange County Superior Court, Edmond was only peripherally aware of the people around him in the gallery. When he'd entered, he'd recognized witnesses from the trial and some news reporters. The only person who mattered right now, however, was the middle-aged man in a robe seated behind the bench.

By now, the judge would have reviewed the presentencing reports and statements. Surely they mentioned that Barbara had no prior criminal record. Yet although Edmond wasn't an expert on body language, to him the judge appeared stern.

After a few introductory remarks, His Honor addressed Barbara directly. "You have been convicted of participating in a robbery spree that endangered both the victims and other bystanders. It also resulted in your partner's death." Near Edmond, a woman nodded agreement. "Although your incarceration will deprive your daughter of her mother's care, it's only by luck that the shootout that killed Mr. Greeley didn't also deprive other children of their parents, or parents of their children."

Edmond's fists tightened. While he couldn't disagree with the judge, this boded ill for his sister.

Briefly, His Honor reviewed the counts on which she'd been convicted. Then he pronounced sentence: six years on each of the three counts of robbery, to be served concurrently.

Six years. While other members of the gallery murmured their approval, Edmond sat motionless, struggling to grasp the implications. Since the law required a felon to serve a minimum of eighty-five percent of the term, Barbara faced five years in prison even if she received a reduction for good behavior.

Edmond had understood there'd been a risk of a long sentence. Yet, emotionally, he'd hoped for a year followed by probation. His backup plan of moving in with Mort and Isabel simply wasn't feasible for longer than a year.

"Six years may seem like an eternity, especially to a

woman your age," the judge continued. "However, this is not only a punishment. It's also a chance to learn from the bad choices that brought you to this point and separated you from your daughter. I hope you'll avail yourself of the educational opportunities in prison and determine to set a better example for your child in the future."

He asked the court clerk to notify the Department of Children and Family Services to check on the daughter's well-being. Edmond felt a wave of gratitude that he already had temporary guardianship and had also filled out the paperwork for permanent guardianship. While a social worker would still have to review Dawn's situation, there was no reason for her to be removed to a foster home.

Dawn. Oh, Lord, how would she take this news?

"You are remanded to the Orange County Jail for transfer to the state Department of Corrections." The judge's severe expression softened. "I wish you luck, Miss Everhart. You still have a chance to make something of your life."

He rose to leave the courtroom. At the defendant's table, Barbara stood along with her attorney. In her orange jumpsuit, she looked small and helpless. Her light brown hair, pulled back in a ponytail, was thin and lank and still held traces of purple dye, a relic of another lifetime.

As the bailiff approached, Barbara turned until her gaze met Edmond's. Tears ran down her cheeks. "Take care of Dawn," she mouthed, and then the bailiff led her away.

"You have to pity her," a woman nearby said to her companion.

"I pity her daughter, not her," the other woman responded. "One of those bullets nearly hit my son."

In the hall, Edmond caught up with the attorney. A man in his mid-forties, Joseph Noriega had a weary air. "I know it isn't what you hoped for, but it's fair," he told Edmond.

"What about an appeal?" Edmond asked. "She has sixty days to file, doesn't she?"

"I'll talk to her," Noriega said. "But I recommend against it."

"Why?" If his sister might have her conviction overturned or her sentence reduced, that was worth pursuing.

"The evidence against her was overwhelming," Noriega explained. "If the conviction is reversed, the district attorney will retry the case. He might aim for the jugular."

"Prosecute her for Simon's death?" To risk a murder conviction was inconceivable.

"That's right." The attorney shifted the position of his briefcase. "As for resentencing, the judge could set her terms to run consecutively instead of concurrently." That would mean eighteen years, also unthinkable.

Nevertheless, Edmond wasn't ready to give up their last glimmer of hope. "It's my sister's decision."

Noriega cleared his throat. "Yes, it is. She doesn't have to decide immediately, but I'll need time to prepare an appeal."

Edmond moved to the next subject on his mind. "Can I talk to her?"

"Not now. The courthouse isn't set up for visits."

"What about once she gets to jail?"

Noriega glanced at his watch. "I doubt you'll be able to see her tonight, but I'll try to arrange a phone call. She should be in state custody by tomorrow."

"Thanks." Edmond knew the man was doing his best. While Noriega might not be a high-flying celebrity defense attorney, he had a solid reputation.

Left alone in the wide corridor, Edmond gathered his thoughts. His father and stepmother would be anxiously waiting for news. Although Isabel had arranged for Dawn to spend the afternoon with friends, she'd be home in a few hours. A smart little girl, she must be aware of what was happening and worried about her mother.

The responsibility for her and for everything that lay

ahead rested on Edmond's shoulders. Barbara's pleading expression in the courtroom remained seared into his heart. Because she was nine years younger, he'd always been protective of her and tried to compensate for their father's absences and their mother's withdrawal. So when Barbara cried, it had often been Edmond who went to soothe her. They'd become close, and even when his responsibilities chafed, he'd tried not to let her down.

She'd never been the eager student that he was. When she entered her teen years, she'd lagged academically just as Edmond became caught up in college and law school. Still, he'd commuted from home, and tried to supervise her homework.

In retrospect, he realized Barb's relationship with their parents had worsened after he moved out and married Melissa, even though their dad had changed jobs to be closer to his family. Naïve and strong-willed, Barbara had been easy prey when she met Simon at the fast-food restaurant where she'd worked after school. Four years older and an ex-con who'd served a term for assault, he'd manipulated Barb into moving in with him. Despite Edmond's protests, their dad had insisted he'd done all he could to rein her in and had refused to call the police. Their mom had pleaded with Edmond not to make waves, afraid Barbara would cut off contact entirely.

I shouldn't have listened. She was underage and he was an ex-con.

But Edmond hadn't fought his parents' decision. As a result, his sister was headed for a long stretch in state prison.

He hoped Noriega could arrange that call tonight. Contact would be difficult after she left the county jail.

Although he didn't often deal with criminal cases, he knew she'd be transferred to a prison reception center for an evaluation that could take weeks. Depending on such factors as the length of her sentence and how big a security risk she posed, she'd then be assigned to an appropriate facility. With luck, she'd serve her term at the women's prison in Fontana, about an hour's drive from Safe Harbor. Once she was transferred, he could arrange regular visits with Dawn.

In the interim, his sister faced a frightening adjustment away from her loved ones, in a strange and intimidating environment over which she had no control. She'd be locked up with gang members, drug users and other women far tougher than she was. Picturing how terrified she must be, Edmond went cold.

From another courtroom, a group of people emerged, possibly jurors being released for the day. He stepped to the side.

But when he took out his phone, he couldn't bring himself to press his parents' number. He needed to figure out how to explain the situation and provide a reassurance he was far from feeling.

If he could just bounce his concerns off someone, someone he trusted with his most sensitive emotions. And only one person fit that description.

MELISSA NEARLY CALLED Edmond several times that afternoon. But much as she was worried about Barbara and Dawn, Edmond had more important matters to deal with. She'd wait and try him later this evening.

Also, concerned about the issues her doctor had raised this morning, she kept an eye on her supervisor's office across the reception area. Jan had been with clients and staffers all afternoon.

Spotting her alone at last, Melissa went to confer with her. Crossing the outer office, she paused when the receptionist asked, "Any word from Edmond about his sister?"

"How do you know about that?" Melissa hadn't discussed Barbara's situation with the young woman, who was noted—or notorious—for tapping into the office grapevine. At times, Melissa suspected Caroline *was* the office grapevine.

"Someone must have mentioned it." She ducked her head. "Honestly, I swore off gossip when the neighbors were jawing about my parents splitting up and I discovered how much it hurt. They're together again, by the way."

"I'm glad. And to answer your question, I haven't heard anything from Edmond today." Melissa edged toward her supervisor's office. "I have to talk to Jan before she takes off again."

"Okay." Caroline spread her hands. "If there's anything I can do, just say the word."

"Thanks." Hurrying away, Melissa tapped on the coordinator's open door, glanced inside for permission and entered.

It didn't take long to sketch the bed rest situation for Jan, which surely she'd expected. Small and intense, Jan Garcia Sargent moved from behind her desk to a chair beside Melissa's.

"I'm delighted that you plan to continue working and consulting as long as possible." After a busy day, Jan's normally smooth dark hair tumbled breezily over her suit collar. "You're an important member of this team. We'll work around your confinement, if I may use such an old-fashioned word. Multiple pregnancies aren't to be taken lightly."

"I wonder if I bit off more than I can chew." Melissa halted, embarrassed to have revealed that. "It's just that I'm a single mom. There's three of them and only one of me."

"I was a single mother, too, although not to triplets," Jan observed. "I only had Kimmie, but my life was a lot more messed up than yours when she was born. Not that yours is messed up."

"I understand." Melissa took no offense.

"This is a rough period, but it will pass." Jan's gaze strayed to a two-part frame on her desk. The faces of her nine-year-old daughter and ten-year-old stepdaughter, Berry, beamed out. "It's worth the sacrifices."

"Still, I feel like I pushed off down a ski slope without realizing how steep it is." *Enough about that.* Melissa shifted to less personal matters. "I'm glad you understand about my work situation."

"Karen and I can handle some of your duties," Jan assured her. "And thank heaven for teleconferencing."

"As long as clients don't mind me being as big as a whale," she said ruefully.

"That's what most of them are hoping will happen to them," Jan reminded her.

"I suppose so." As she took her leave, Melissa felt better. She doubted many bosses—especially those who didn't work in a fertility program—would be as supportive.

It was nearly five o'clock when she returned to her desk. Might as well close up for the day.

Her cell rang. Heart thumping, she glanced at the readout. *Edmond.*

"What happened?' she asked without preamble.

"Six years." His voice shook.

Six years? Barbara would be thirty when she was released. Melissa ached for her former sister-in-law and for Dawn. "Is she all right?"

"I imagine she's in shock," he said. "In retrospect, I should have been prepared for it, but this is hard for me to accept."

His honesty meant a lot. In the past, he'd had a tendency to put up a brave front, even when she'd suspected he felt otherwise. "How did your parents take it?"

"I haven't filled them in yet. I'm still at the courthouse."

He'd called her first? This news must have jolted him to the core. And he'd reached out to her, of all people.

"It will be easier if I break the news face to face," Edmond said. "We have a lot of decisions to make."

Underneath the statement, Melissa detected a plea for help. Nurturing her friends and especially Edmond had always satisfied a profound need in her, and she couldn't refuse him now.

"Do you want me to come with you?" Although her only contact with her in-laws since the divorce had been to exchange Christmas cards, she doubted they'd mind.

In spite of everything, she still felt a part of this family. They'd meant so much to her after she lost her own parents.

"Yes!" He sounded relieved. "I value your perspective and I think they would, too."

"Do they still live in the same place? I could meet you there."

"I'd rather we drove together so we can talk en route." He named a restaurant where she could safely leave her car near the courthouse in Santa Ana, which lay about a third of the distance between Safe Harbor and Norwalk.

"I'll get there as soon as I can."

"I'll be waiting."

What did it mean that he'd called her first? Melissa mused as she locked her desk. Nothing, she told herself. In a crisis, people pulled together and set their differences aside.

She hurried out to her car.

Chapter Seven

Edmond's new car—new since the divorce, anyway—was a black sedan that suited him, Melissa reflected as she slid into the cushiony passenger seat. High-tech and well engineered, it was sophisticated yet down-to-earth.

In the enclosed space, his light spicy aroma surrounded her. Inhaling it, she instinctively relaxed.

"Thanks for joining me." Edmond waited while she adjusted the seat belt around herself before shifting into Drive. "My mind keeps running in circles. I hate things being so out of control."

"I understand." Melissa didn't mention the red rim around his eyes. Had he been crying, or had he merely worn his contact lenses earlier? He rarely wore them, since they caused irritation.

Edmond eased the car up a ramp onto the freeway. With the traffic lighter than usual for a weekday rush hour, the navigation computer estimated their trip at twenty minutes.

"My parents fixed up a bedroom for Dawn," he began. "She and Barbara have been staying with them, so she's comfortable there."

"Is that where she lived while she was in school?" Being spared a change of schools would be a plus if her grandparents pressed to keep her with them.

"No, my sister and Simon had an apartment, or rather, several. They moved a lot, probably because they were behind on the rent." Then he added, "With Isabel and Mort, she has a real home, although it's relatively new to her. It may not be wise to uproot her."

"But you have guardianship," Melissa reminded him.

"I have emergency temporary guardianship, but the court could transfer that to her grandparents, if it's for the best." Edmond spoke as if examining the possibilities from all angles.

His attitude disappointed Melissa. She'd observed at the wedding how much Dawn trusted him. But then, he'd sacrificed their marriage rather than become a father.

Striving for a low-key approach, she said, "I'm sure her grandparents dote on her. Still, your dad was never the warm fuzzy type."

"Isabel makes up for that."

"In some respects." A kindly divorcée with no children, Isabel had been a nurse's aide who'd attended Edmond's mother as she lay dying of cancer. Six months later, when Mort Everhart married her, Melissa had been happy for them both.

"We have to act fast," Edmond continued, transitioning into the carpool lane. "I presume family services will be preparing a report and it's best if we can show a stable living environment."

"What kind of report will it be?" Melissa asked.

"A credit and criminal background check on all adults who'll be supervising her, for starters." In the open lane, he stepped harder on the gas. "The state has to ensure that prisoners' children are safe."

"Will there be a home visit?" In connection with her work, Melissa was familiar with procedures in adoption cases, where home studies were required.

"Probably, and they'll interview any adults involved in her care." Edmond grimaced. "When I laid out the procedures for clients, I never understood how intrusive it feels."

Melissa's thoughts turned to the little girl's emotional reaction to her mother's sentencing. "Did you and her therapist discuss how to explain about prison to Dawn?"

He slanted her a smile. "You ask the right questions. Yes, we did go over that. Also, the counselor, Franca Brightman, gave me a list of what children need when their parents are incarcerated."

"What's on the list?" Melissa had never before known a parent or child facing such a situation.

"What you'd expect, for the most part." A freeway sign indicated they were entering Los Angeles County. "To receive full information about what's happening and how it will affect them. To feel safe and be able to express their emotions openly. To understand that they can stay in touch with their parent."

"Is that possible? I mean, on a regular basis." There must be a way to visit Barb, although the impression Melissa had from TV shows involved clanging prison doors, body searches and Plexiglas barriers. How intimidating for a small child. *Or an adult.*

"Yes, we'll work it out once she's assigned to a specific facility," he said. "Right now, though, Barbara's in transition."

"Poor kid." Although Melissa knew her former sister-in-law was in her twenties, she still pictured Barbara as a teenager.

"Her poor daughter," Edmond said. "Sessions with a therapist, visits to Mom in prison, living with relatives. That's hardly a normal childhood."

"Children adjust." That's what Melissa had heard, anyway. "I'm grateful that my parents were wonderful. I had it easy."

"Did you?" He shot her a skeptical look. "They never recovered from your brother's drowning when he was a toddler. It felt to me like they tiptoed around you, and each other."

Melissa hadn't considered how much her childhood had been shaped by the tragedy that had occurred when she was five and Jamie only two. She'd taken her family's tensions for granted. "That's true, I suppose."

"But as you say, you adjusted."

Now that he brought it up, she could see the pattern she'd adopted. "I went to great lengths to avoid conflict, or any behavior that might upset my folks." They'd never talked about Jamie, and only years later had her mother shared how much she regretted letting grief and guilt dissuade her from having another baby.

"We both took on the role of good child," Edmond noted. "We tried to protect our own parents."

"That's true. We had a lot in common." Melissa sometimes forgot how similar they'd been in most respects.

Edmond concentrated on the road ahead as they exited the freeway. A wide boulevard led through the business district of Norwalk, a city of about a hundred thousand people. A few signal lights later, he followed a series of side streets lined with unpretentious homes until they reached the place Melissa remembered well, a one-story house with a small, patchy lawn.

As Edmond parked, she took in the fading paint and scrubby bushes. She didn't recall the place having such a tired appearance.

On the sidewalk, Melissa started to reach for his hand, then thought better of it. Much as she longed to help Edmond, she was only here as an observer.

For his sake, she hoped he and his parents could figure out what was best for Dawn.

WHEN PRESENTING OPTIONS to clients for divorces, custody issues or other family matters, Edmond prepared thoroughly.

As a result, he was accustomed to experiencing a sense of calm as he geared up for action.

Not today. Although his initial near-panic had abated, he had to focus on breathing regularly as he rang the doorbell. Reviewing the situation with Melissa had reinforced his conviction that Dawn belonged with his father and stepmother, yet an undercurrent of uneasiness remained.

Inside, the floor creaked and the door unlatched to reveal Isabel Everhart, her stocky figure still robust at age sixty-three and her brown hair only lightly touched with gray. Her gaze moved past Edmond to Melissa. "Well, this is a nice surprise."

"I'm glad to be here." Melissa reached to hug her former mother-in-law. "Edmond and I are coworkers at the hospital now—I'm sure he told you that."

"He didn't tell me about this." Ushering them inside, Isabel patted Melissa's bulge.

"Long story," she said apologetically.

"I wasn't asking." Isabel had always respected other people's privacy. It was one of the many qualities Edmond liked about her.

"I wouldn't blame you if you did," Melissa said. "But we have more important things to talk about today."

"Yes, we do."

In the living room, Edmond's father clicked off the TV and arose from the well-worn couch. In his late sixties, he had thinning white hair and weathered skin, the deep creases testifying to years of smoking. He'd quit during his first wife's final illness.

"About time you got here," he grumbled to Edmond. To Melissa, he said, "Dare I hope my son finally showed some smarts and won you back?"

"It's good to see you, too, Mort." She shared a light hug with the old man.

"You're together again?" He'd always had a soft spot for his daughter-in-law.

"We're friends, that's all." Edmond didn't want his ex-wife's presence to distract them. "Dad, Isabel…"

"If you didn't knock her up, who did?" Mort demanded.

"That's none of our business." Isabel spoke more forcefully than usual. "Edmond, the lawyer called and broke the news about the sentence."

Damn. He'd waited too long. "That should have come from me. I assumed this might be easier in person."

"None of this is easy," Mort growled.

"That's neither here nor there." Isabel continued briskly, "Mr. Noriega said he'll have Barbara call you in about a quarter of an hour, and Dawn should be home any minute. We'd better talk fast."

Edmond agreed. "Okay. About where Dawn's going to live…"

"I haven't had dessert," Mort growled. "Be in the kitchen." With that, he stomped off.

Although his dad had never been the sociable type, this was abrupt even for him. "He must be angry about the sentence. Or at Barbara," Edmond guessed.

"Both, I suppose, but that's not the whole story." His stepmother took a seat in a flowered armchair, leaving the couch to her guests. "I'll be frank with you."

"Please do." Now what? Edmond was grateful for Melissa sitting quietly beside him, hands folded in her lap.

"I know we discussed keeping Dawn here, but that's no longer possible," Isabel said.

Perhaps she didn't understand how much support Edmond planned to provide, both financially and in practical terms. "This is a longer sentence than we expected," he conceded. "However, I can arrange things…"

"Hear me out." Isabel didn't sound angry. In fact, he'd

have pegged her emotion as sadness. "I have something to tell you."

"Is it Dad's cancer?" Edmond had believed that was no longer a threat.

"No." In the early-evening light through the window, his stepmother's square, plain face showed a sprinkling of age spots. "But Mort's oncologist observed some behaviors that concerned him and referred us to a specialist."

"Behaviors?" Edmond queried.

"Your father is showing signs of dementia."

In the shocked silence that followed, Edmond became aware of random noises—the hum of electricity, the rattle of a truck on a nearby street, a dog barking in a neighbor's yard. "I wish you'd said something to me earlier." He'd assumed they were keeping him in the loop.

"We just found out this morning," Isabel said.

"I'm so sorry." Melissa regarded her in dismay. "What a horrible thing. And the timing is terrible."

No wonder Mort had left the room before this discussion. "How severe is this? Is it Alzheimer's?" Edmond asked.

"Too soon to be sure." Isabel swallowed. "We're arranging for further testing."

"How's Dad taking it?"

"He rejects the whole idea." His stepmother shrugged. "Claims he's fine."

"That's natural," Melissa said. "It's a scary diagnosis."

"There's no actual diagnosis yet," Isabel corrected. "Just a suspicion."

"He has to face up to this." Edmond had heard that with dementia, early treatment could make a big difference.

"Face up to losing his grip on reality? His memories, his personality?" Isabel's voice broke.

"You're right." Until now, Edmond hadn't viewed this development from his parents' perspective. "It's devastating news."

"We're taking it one day at a time." His stepmother sighed. "Obviously, we can't raise a child under these circumstances. She'll have to live with you."

Dawn deserved a nurturing home with experienced adults. She faced a difficult adjustment. What chance did she have with an uncle who'd failed miserably when he'd tried to be there for his sister?

Edmond had confidence in his ability to handle challenges at work and in court. But when it came to raising a child, he was lost. If he failed Dawn—if she grew up consumed by anger, or so desperate for masculine attention that she ran to a man like her father—it would be even worse than what had happened with Barbara. He'd have no one to share the guilt with. The entire responsibility would fall on him.

Around him, the silence lengthened, and he appreciated the women's willingness to let him struggle with his inner turmoil. Ultimately, what choice was there? Edmond had promised to supervise his niece's care if necessary. And necessary it seemed to be.

Outside, a car door slammed and a childish voice called her thanks to someone. "She's home," Isabel said, unnecessarily.

He'd run out of time.

"No!" More like a two-year-old than a seven-year-old, Dawn thrust out her lower lip, folded her arms and sat rigid on her chair. "I can't go live with Uncle Eddie."

Melissa noted the frustrated exchange of looks between Edmond and Isabel. They'd spent the past few minutes gently explaining about the sentence and assuring the little girl that she'd be safe and happy with her uncle.

"I'll rent a larger place where you can have your own bedroom." Edmond was hiding his doubts well, in Melissa's opinion. "You'll enjoy Safe Harbor. Remember how much fun you had at the wedding?"

"You can take your furniture with you," Isabel added. "And of course your books and toys."

"No." The little girl blinked back tears.

"Honey, Grandpa Mort has serious health problems." Isabel peered toward the kitchen, but there was no sign of the old man. "And your uncle loves you."

"A lot," Edmond added.

"I love you, too, but I can't live with you." Dawn hunkered down. Even her short brown hair seemed to bristle with defiance.

Melissa glanced worriedly at Edmond. She knew it had been hard enough for him to accept his role as surrogate parent without this rebelliousness.

However, only the tightness around his mouth revealed his impatience. "All these changes are a lot for you to accept, sweetheart. But I'm not such a bad guy, am I?"

"No." She sniffled.

"You can stay with Grandpa and me for a week or two, until your uncle's prepared a place for you," Isabel assured her. "That'll give you a chance to wrap your mind around this."

"I can't!" More quietly, Dawn said, "I'm going to prison with Mommy."

Her innocent loyalty brought Melissa near tears. What a brave little soul her niece was.

"Whatever gave you that idea?" Isabel shook her head in dismissal.

"They don't allow that," Edmond said edgily. "None of us is happy about this long sentence, Dawn, but we have to adapt."

"I *am* adapting!" she insisted. "I'll wear an orange jumpsuit like prisoners on TV."

"This isn't a game of dress-up. You can't play pretend prisoner." At Edmond's sharp tone, the little girl cringed.

Melissa had tried to stay out of the discussion. The problem was that, in their different ways, both Edmond and Isabel were so intent on persuading Dawn to accept the inevitable that neither questioned the cause of her stubbornness.

"Dawn, of course you're upset about your mommy." Melissa gazed into the little girl's misty eyes. "But why should you go to prison with her?"

"If I'm not there, who'll take care of her?" The question emerged breathlessly.

"What do you mean?" Edmond asked.

"She skips breakfast," Dawn said earnestly. "She forgets to put the laundry in the dryer."

"Believe me, in prison that won't be a problem," he muttered.

"You can't be sure of that!"

He frowned. "I'm a lawyer, honey. I'm aware of how prisons operate."

He was missing the emotional context, Melissa thought, and spoke again. "Dawn, do you believe it's your job to take care of your mom?"

"Somebody has to," she said. "I'll stay with her. I don't mind."

"Prisons aren't for children." Edmond spoke more gently.

"You could ask them," Dawn responded.

Melissa stroked the child's hair. "It's loving of you to try, but your mom's grown-up. She has to take care of herself now."

"And prisons are very well run. They have kitchens and laundry rooms and— Hold on." Edmond drew his vibrating phone from his pocket. "Yes, Mr. Noriega? Thank you! Of course I'll talk to her."

The attorney must be about to put Barbara on the line.

Melissa hoped her sister-in-law wasn't in meltdown. That would only make things harder for Dawn.

Edmond carried the phone into the hall. As the little girl jumped up, Isabel touched her granddaughter's arm. "Give them a minute, sweetie."

Dawn plopped down again. Lips pressed together in a firm line, she sat shaking with tension.

Chapter Eight

"In court, I could tell the audience was pleased about the sentence." On the phone, Barbara's words rang with pain. "It's awful how close those bullets came to hitting bystanders. I screwed up. I guess I deserve this. But I'm scared, Eddie."

"Has anyone hurt or threatened you?" he asked, careful to face away from the living room to prevent his voice from carrying.

"No, but in this place they're taking me to, I'm sure there'll be women who've done all sorts of things. I've seen prison movies."

He pictured his little sister's frightened green eyes, much like Dawn's. "Remember what I told you before. Be polite to everyone and don't make friends or enemies. Don't ask questions or accept favors." Behind bars, there were different rules of social behavior. "I'll arrange to visit as soon as possible."

She hurried on. "Don't bring Dawn till I'm assigned somewhere. At the reception center, I'm not allowed to touch anyone, and it would drive us both crazy. Mr. Noriega said I can't have phone calls while I'm there, either, just paper to write letters. Oh, I wish I could hug her!"

"She's worried about you." That was an understatement, he thought. "Seeing you might reassure her."

"Or terrify her. She has to get used to her new life. Please keep a close watch on her. Isabel means well, but…" The sentence trailed off.

"Isabel has her hands full with Dad." Edmond summarized their father's tentative diagnosis. "I'm sorry to drop this on you. I'm sure you wish you could be here for him."

"Isabel will cope fine," Barbara said. "You'll take care of Dawn as you promised, won't you?"

There was no room for hesitation. "Absolutely," he said. "As soon as I find a bigger apartment, she'll move in with me."

"You'll be a great dad."

His sister was overestimating his abilities. "I don't understand children," Edmond admitted. "Melissa's much better with her than I am."

"Melissa's there?"

"She came with me today," he confirmed.

"That's wonderful. I was hoping you'd reconnect." Barbara had been enthusiastic on Saturday morning when he'd mentioned having run into his ex-wife.

No sense emphasizing that he and Melissa were merely friends. He hadn't brought up the pregnancy, either, and wasn't about to now. "She's very fond of her niece."

A small figure darted into the hallway. "Can I talk to Mommy?" Dawn demanded.

"My baby!" Barbara cried in Edmond's ear.

"I'll put you on speaker." He tapped the phone. "Go ahead."

From the front room, Melissa ventured into view, arms folded over her middle. They shared an apprehensive look as Dawn blurted, "I want to go with you, Mommy. Where are you?"

"Honey, I miss you." Despite a catch in her voice, Barbara forged on. "Mommy did wrong. I broke the law and I can't be with you for a while. Uncle Eddie and Aunt Lissa are there. You behave."

Dawn broke into tears. "Mommy, you need me!"

Still holding out the phone, Edmond wrapped an arm around her. "It's okay, sweetheart. I'm here."

"Dawn, it's the grown-ups' job to take care of you." Barbara spoke with more maturity than he'd heard from her before.

"Who's going to cook for you?" the little girl persisted.

"They serve regular meals in prison. It's like having my own restaurant."

"What about your dirty clothes?" Dawn asked.

"Prisons have a laundry." Barbara assured her. "Honey, until we can visit again, I'll write you letters, real letters, not email. You can practice reading them."

As his sister struggled to put up a brave front for her daughter, Edmond's chest squeezed.

"I'll write you, too, Mommy," Dawn said. "Aunt Lissa, will you help me?"

"Of course," Melissa assured her. "We can send pictures, too."

"Mel? I'm glad you're there. Oh, damn, I have to go." Barbara sniffled. "I love you all. Eddie, take care of my baby."

"I will." His breath came fast but he held his emotions in check. No sense in all of them breaking down.

After a round of farewells, the call ended. Edmond flashed on a memory of his sister at about Dawn's age. Sixteen and newly licensed, he'd picked her up one day after school.

Beaming, she'd bounced in her seat as he drove at a snail's pace, stopping at every yellow light and signaling for a quarter mile before each turn. "Go faster!" she'd cried.

"Drivers have to obey the speed limit," he'd said.

"Nobody's watching."

"That isn't the point. I might I hit someone." Even as a teenager, he'd had a strong awareness of consequences.

"You won't," she'd responded confidently.

"I won't because I'll be careful not to."

She'd laughed. "You should have more fun, Eddie."

They'd had contrasting personalities from the start. Sadly, she hadn't learned from his example or from her own experiences. Now she was paying a high price for her recklessness.

So was her daughter, Edmond reflected, holding Dawn close while sobs racked her little body. Prepared or not, he'd become her guardian in every sense.

He hadn't been able to save his sister. He hoped he'd do better for his niece.

MELISSA HAD ALWAYS been organized. On school nights, she'd laid out the next day's clothes over a chair and placed her books and homework in her backpack. She'd also maintained a wall calendar where she'd tracked upcoming tests and field trips. Friends had considered her weird, but her parents had approved.

Being on top of things had felt right. Sudden changes of plan, however, had distressed her unduly. Suffering stomach flu the morning of a math test, she'd hidden her symptoms from her mother and thrown up in the school hallway. Seeing her mother's worry when she'd arrived to take her home, Melissa had burst into tears.

It's okay to get sick, her mom had said. *Everybody does.*

Melissa hadn't shared the fear that gripped her because she hadn't clearly understood it herself. Losing control meant spinning loose without a mooring. Organization was her coping strategy, her security.

Once, just once, her mom had failed to watch two-year-old Jamie as closely as usual. At a neighbor's house during a party, he'd fallen into the swimming pool. He hadn't cried out or thrashed in the water, and no one had noticed. It had been Melissa, only a few years older, who'd spotted his little body at the bottom of the pool. The sight had been so sur-real, she'd had to look twice before she started screaming.

Later, she'd tormented herself, wondering if he could have been saved had she reacted sooner. That fear had per-sisted for years, and she'd realized later that it had contrib-uted to her sense that she'd be happiest without children. Only after a confidence from her mother, shortly before her parents' deaths, had Melissa released that nagging guilt and been able to acknowledge her deep desire to be a parent.

She understood Dawn's wish to accompany her mother behind bars. Some kids felt they were to blame for anything that went wrong around them. She figured it was even more true in a dysfunctional household, where the child might assume an adult role as a coping mechanism. In Edmond's home, with his father often away and his mother rather pas-sive, he'd believed it was up to him to supervise his sister.

In the car, Melissa studied Edmond's profile as he navi-gated the freeway on-ramp.

"I admire you for taking in your niece," she said. "I know how hard it is for you."

He gripped the steering wheel. "Part of me is angry with Barbara, even though I feel rotten about what's happened."

Melissa watched him intently. "This situation isn't fair to you or to Dawn."

Seconds ticked by while he merged into traffic, which had thinned as rush hour passed and twilight descended. "I'll do everything I can, but is it really best for her to live with an uncle who has no idea how to be a dad?"

"I'm no expert on being a mom, either," she pointed out. "Especially to triplets. But my friends assure me you get on-the-job training. Plus, there's no single way to be a parent. Every person is different, although there are ground rules."

"Like feeding them and washing their clothes?" he asked dryly.

"And holding them when they cry," she said. "You've already mastered that part."

He shrugged. "I can do the obvious stuff, but I lack the right instincts."

She weighed her words, wary of pushing too hard. "There's a learning curve for everyone. But you *are* sensitive to your niece."

"Not as sensitive as you. Would you be willing...?" He cleared his throat. "I hate to impose, but can you help while we settle in? I'm a bit overwhelmed by what lies ahead, and Dawn's attached to you."

Despite Dr. Sargent's cautions and her awareness that she'd soon have to limit her activities, Melissa's spirits rose at the request. Being able to nurture others had always been central to her happiness, and at this crisis point, both Edmond and Dawn clearly needed her.

"Of course." She shifted in her seat to ease the tugging of her abdominal muscles.

"It's only for a few days," Edmond went on. "I should draw up a parenting plan, the way I advise my clients to do in a custody situation."

"Smart idea." Being a family attorney had prepared him in a lot of ways, at least for the practical aspects of his new role.

Edmond shook his head. "On top of everything else, I'm worried about Dad."

"Dementia is terrifying." Melissa would prefer a physical disease, however deadly, to mental deterioration, but people didn't get the choice. "However, it will probably develop gradually, and Isabel's handling the doctor appointments. Let's stick to what has to be done right away."

"You always anchor me." Edmond slowed to let a truck shift into their lane.

"Glad to do it."

He flicked on the car lights in the growing darkness.

"To begin with, I'll have to rent a bigger apartment with a bedroom for Dawn."

"What about a house?" Melissa recalled her receptionist mentioning a three-bedroom place for rent down the block from her family's home. "I heard of a vacancy a mile or so from the hospital."

"I'd like a house." The tension in Edmond's shoulders eased. "Compared to an apartment, a house has a greater sense of permanence, and a yard to play in."

Taking out her phone, Melissa opened the organizer. "I'll start a list."

He gave her a crooked grin. "You and your lists."

"You do the same thing!"

"We have that in common," he agreed. "Will you send it to me when we're done?"

"No, I was planning to keep it to myself and charge you for access," she teased.

His answering chuckle warmed her. "Okay, let's have at it. Put down renting a house. I should buy more household supplies, too. I'm always running out of detergent—I certainly don't want Dawn assuming she's responsible for *my* laundry now."

"Don't forget about day care." Melissa recalled a nurse discussing her child's activities. "The community college runs a summer sports camp for kids, with two-week sessions. At Dawn's age, that should be more interesting than parking her in the hospital's child center."

"I'm not sure she's the athletic type," Edmond said. "Barbara never talked about that."

"Sports camp offers gymnastics, swimming and other fun stuff geared to little kids," she said. "I can check it out online."

"I don't mean to lay too much on you," he cautioned. "Especially in your condition."

"Mostly I'll handle things from home." Melissa jotted

another note. "You'll have to enroll her in school soon. It starts in August."

"I'll discuss that with Geoff Humphreys's wife. She teaches second grade." Keeping his gaze on the road, he said, "I'm glad you're tracking all this."

"Thumbs of steel," she kidded as she pressed the tiny buttons.

"Oh, and remind me to keep tabs on Barbara's status," he said. "We'll visit as soon as she's placed."

"Got it."

"I should stay in touch with her lawyer about an appeal, too," he went on. "He recommends against it. Still, she has sixty days to decide."

The list was lengthening, and Melissa hadn't finished. "I'll check with Isabel about Dawn's favorite foods."

"Ouch. Meal preparation is *not* my strong point." Beneath his glasses, Edmond rolled his eyes. "Please don't tell me to take a cooking class."

"Just hang out at my house," she assured him. "You'll learn by osmosis."

"Your roommates wouldn't mind?"

"They like Dawn. And you, too." Melissa suspected the group would enjoy teaching Edmond to fix meals for his niece. "It's fun when there are guests at meals."

"I'll chip in for the cost, of course."

"Definitely."

Ideas flowed between them. Maintain Dawn's schedule with her counselor. Contact child services and provide information for the social worker's report. Use Isabel's email address to provide daily updates to her and Dawn about their preparations so the little girl felt involved in the process.

At the same time, a cloud of "if-onlys" swarmed inside Melissa's head. If only Edmond hadn't refused to consider parenthood, they'd still be together. If only they'd had a baby, they could welcome Dawn into an established family. If only his heart had room enough for a houseful of babies.

What a ridiculous notion. She was projecting her longings onto a man who'd made his position crystal clear.

For the few weeks remaining before she had to restrict her activities, she'd do her best to serve as Dawn's aunt and Edmond's friend. She'd be a fool to fantasize about anything more.

She would never allow him, or her own vulnerability, to break her heart again. That didn't mean she had to abandon him or her niece.

She was stronger now than she'd been during their marriage, Melissa reflected. And surrounded by friends.

THEY WERE ON a roll. Edmond's spirits, which had hit bottom after his sister's conviction, resurged. Not that he underestimated the difficulties ahead, but he'd regained a sense of order, thanks in large part to Melissa.

Stealing a glance at her, he admired the luxurious flow of her fair hair and the velvety texture of her skin illuminated by passing car lights. The adjectives he associated with her—*graceful* and *radiant*—were especially apt since her pregnancy.

Yet a question nagged at him, one that he should have asked years ago. Raising it now might roil the waters, but it lay between them, a thin, nearly invisible barrier that blocked any possibility of drawing closer.

"Mel," he said. "May I ask you something?"

She must have registered the difference in his tone, because she set her phone in her lap. "Shoot."

"I never understood why you changed your mind about having children." He didn't wish to provoke an argument, but a sense of fairness propelled him to clarify, "You always seemed as happy as I was with our marriage."

"Lots of women change their position on motherhood

when they get older." Despite the defensive words, she sounded more introspective than angry. "You've heard of the infamous biological clock. And because I work in the fertility field, I'm around babies and maternal hormones. They have a powerful effect."

That was the explanation she'd given previously. It hadn't satisfied him then and it didn't now. "There had to be more. You just sprang it on me."

She gave a startled jerk. "No, I didn't."

"It was as if you turned thirty and suddenly I hardly recognized you." He tried not to sound accusatory.

"I didn't spring it on you," she said. "We'd discussed having children."

"When?"

"After my parents died." That had been several years before they split up.

Vaguely, Edmond remembered her talking about the meaning of parenthood, but he'd associated that with the shock of losing her parents in a car accident while the couple was vacationing in Hawaii. "Maybe in the theoretical sense."

"It was more than that," Melissa insisted. "We talked about regrets, about not being able to go back and undo our choices." She had a much sharper memory of this conversation than he did, Edmond gathered.

"And that related to having children?" He'd failed to grasp the implication.

"I cited parenthood as an example of things we might regret."

"As I said, it was a theoretical discussion." Freeway lights banished the darkness as they neared the restaurant where Melissa had left her car. "Then you dropped it."

"Not exactly." She adjusted the seat belt, which kept slipping around her bulge. "I didn't want to hammer too hard because your mom was sick."

That failed to explain her abrupt insistence on having children. "If it mattered that much to you, you should have pursued it, not ambushed me with it."

"What difference would it have made?"

Acting evasive was out of character for her. "There's something you're not saying."

"Stop interrogating me. We aren't in court."

Edmond's marriage, his vision of the future and his happiness had crashed because of his wife's sudden demand. Granted, he'd contributed to the mess with his high-handed response, but the discovery that she was hiding her reasons, or a significant part of them, disturbed him.

"Tell me what you withheld," he said. "Please."

He'd gained enough perspective to understand that she instinctively avoided conflict. That hadn't usually been a problem between them, but in the grip of strong emotions, he must have spoken more forcefully than he intended.

This time, Edmond resolved to listen carefully. But he wouldn't let up until she told the whole truth.

Chapter Nine

Distressed, Melissa shook her head. "I can't."

"Not acceptable." He'd read once that you had to clean out a wound before you had any chance at healing. That struck him as true for relationships, too. "Married couples aren't supposed to keep secrets."

"It wasn't my secret to keep."

What an odd statement. "Whose was it?"

"My mother's."

How could a secret of her mother's have destroyed their marriage? he wondered as he exited the freeway. "Melissa, she's not in a place where she needs you to protect her anymore."

She shivered as if her mother were watching from beyond the grave. "I promised never to betray her confidence."

"This is ridiculous." Hearing the dismissiveness in his voice, Edmond amended, "I understand that you're upset. But I have a stake in this, too."

For a moment, the only noises were the rush of traffic and a siren wailing in the distance. Finally she spoke.

"Before they left for Hawaii, Mom apologized to me." She swallowed. "She knew how traumatic it had been for me, discovering my baby brother's body at the bottom of a pool."

He hadn't heard that part of the story. "I didn't realize you were the one who found him."

"I spotted him under the water. It was surreal, like a bad dream." Melissa took a couple of breaths before continuing. "I had nightmares."

"I can imagine. Did you get therapy?"

"No, and Dad was a psychologist. Isn't that ironic?" She shook her head. "For years, Mom refused to discuss anything about that day. She believed it was her fault because she didn't watch Jamie closely enough."

"Any parent would, I expect." Edmond had handled several divorces in which one partner blamed the other for the serious injury or death of a child. Sometimes they blamed themselves.

"It was more than that." She paused.

Aware of her emotional struggle, he quashed the urge to prod her for how her family's long-ago tragedy had affected her desire for parenthood. He *had* learned something in their three years apart.

"My mother explained that, at the pool party, the hosts were fixing margaritas. Mom rarely drank, but she didn't taste much alcohol in the margaritas, so she had several," Melissa said. "She wasn't sure how many. Three or four."

"That's why she wasn't watching Jamie closely," he guessed.

"Yes. The guilt haunted her." Tilting her head back, Melissa closed her eyes. Picturing her mother's face? Mary Fenton had been a classic beauty like her daughter, but she'd had deep-etched lines around her mouth and eyes. "Dad urged her to have another baby, but to her the risk was intolerable."

"You believe she was punishing herself?"

"Maybe, or terrified of screwing up again," Melissa replied. "After we were married and I made it clear we didn't plan on having kids, she feared her negative attitude had poisoned me against motherhood."

"Had it?" While she mulled his question, Edmond turned onto the street leading to the restaurant and swung into the parking lot. A scattering of cars bordered the coffee shop, with Melissa's white sedan sitting slightly apart. He pulled into an adjacent space and cut the engine.

"In retrospect, yes. After that conversation, I started to reevaluate my assumptions," Melissa said. "I talked about it to you a little, but then we got the news that they'd been killed. We were just recovering from that when your mom's cancer entered the terminal stage. There was a lot going on."

That might explain why he'd overlooked her subtle clues about motherhood. "I didn't notice a change in you, beyond what one might expect from losing loved ones."

"I wasn't entirely aware of it myself," Melissa conceded. "But I began to find kids fascinating. I realized that at some level, I had blamed myself, too, for not responding faster when I saw Jamie under the water. It was only a matter of seconds, but it felt like minutes. Somehow Mom's confession took that guilt away."

"So when you agreed with me that kids weren't necessary for a happy marriage," Edmond said slowly, "underneath that you were really afraid you couldn't protect them." He understood her fears, considering his regrets about not intervening with Barbara.

"I guess so, but I hated to cause problems in our marriage, particularly at such a difficult time for you. For a while I figured this desire for a baby would pass, so I tried not to dwell on it," Melissa admitted.

"What pushed you over the edge?" He assumed there'd been a trigger.

"One day at the lab where I worked, a woman who'd been on maternity leave brought in her baby." Melissa unsnapped her seat belt. "She offered to let me hold him. Feeling his little body in my arms, inhaling his baby scent, I just…I understood that having children was the reason I was put on this earth. That discovery must have been building inside me, but it hadn't hit me until then, and when it did, I had to share it with you right away. I suppose I should have eased into the conversation with more care."

A chill ran through Edmond. *That* conversation remained burned into his memory. "To me, your announcement came out of nowhere. It was as if you rejected everything we'd built together. As if you rejected *me*."

She stared at him, aghast. "I assumed it would bring us closer together."

"How could you imagine that?"

"I figured that once you got used to the idea, you'd be as excited about the new adventure as I was." She swallowed hard. "It meant so much to me, and then you went out and destroyed any possibility of compromise."

"Compromise?" Edmond didn't see how one could compromise on the subject. "You either have children or you don't."

"I believed you would discover that you'd grown, that you'd…matured since we first talked about kids."

Despite his resolve to listen patiently, he couldn't let the remark pass. "That's unfair. My decision not to have children *was* a mature one, based on my experience and my beliefs—beliefs we both held." His old anguish still burned. "When you changed your mind, you basically chose motherhood over me."

"When you had a vasectomy, you chose childlessness over *me*," she answered unhappily.

"That's not what I meant at all. I *was* choosing you, I was choosing the happy life that we shared.."

"To me, it seemed like I'd shared what mattered most to me, and you threw it in my face. How could I ever trust you again?" Melissa scooped her purse off the floor. "It's too late to undo any of this, even if we wanted to."

Edmond's chest hurt. More than that, his entire body hurt. Yet unfortunately, she was right. It was too late. "I hope we can still cooperate for Dawn's sake."

"Certainly." She opened her door. "We just have to keep our emotions out of it."

"And if you need anything during your pregnancy, don't hesitate to call me." Edmond knew she was facing serious challenges.

"Thanks." She stepped out into the night and walked to her car.

Sitting there and mentally replaying the conversation, he wished he'd grasped her perspective at the time. He wouldn't have arbitrarily obtained a vasectomy—that had been arrogant. Still, it was doubtful their marriage could have survived. Edmond didn't want to be a father. He loved Dawn and he'd do his best as her guardian. But that didn't make him daddy material.

He waited while Melissa started her car and backed out. Then he followed the white sedan onto the freeway, watching over her until their paths diverged in Safe Harbor.

They might have no hope of reconciliation, but he still cared about her safety. He still cared about her.

Tuesday afternoon

Sender: Edmond Everhart
Subject: Our new home
Cc: Melissa Everhart

Dear Dawn and Isabel,
At lunch today, Aunt Lissa and I visited two houses for rent in Safe Harbor. One is a cottage near the beach, with a

small yard and two bedrooms. The other has three bedrooms and a nicer yard and patio, but it's farther from the beach. I'm attaching pictures. Which looks better to you? I can't guarantee we'll get your pick, but I'll try.

Also, is it okay if I sign you up for sports camp during the day, while I'm working? You can play games and go swimming. Everyone says it's fun.

Love, Uncle Eddie

"I'd pick the house with more space," remarked legal secretary Lisa Rosen, removing a yogurt from the refrigerator in the law firm's lunchroom. Edmond had shared the pictures with the staff, who took a keen interest in his domestic situation.

"It's smart to include your niece in the process," added the fiftyish receptionist, Marie Belasco, who was replacing coffee supplies in the cabinet. "Fresh pot will be ready in a minute."

"I've had too much caffeine today anyway." Edmond had been running on full speed since early morning, returning phone calls and preparing pleadings for clients while starting on the list of things Dawn would need. He'd emailed Children and Family Services to ask the name of the social worker and checked out the sports camp website. Melissa had been a champ, setting up their lunchtime tour of rentals and accompanying him.

They were an effective team. He'd observed the overall condition of the houses, the square footage and the floor plans. She'd noticed the state of the kitchen appliances, the color schemes and the ages of the children playing in the neighborhood.

"The best houses go fast, so don't delay." Lisa, tanned and slim as befitted a sailing enthusiast, leaned against the counter while opening the carton. "Have you talked to

Paula about registering Dawn for school yet? My son Fred was in Paula's class last year and she's fantastic."

"I plan to." Until recently, Edmond hadn't paid much attention to his coworkers' family situations. Now he could reel off the statistics: Lisa and her husband, both in their thirties, had a son and daughter ages eight and ten; Marie was divorced and an experienced foster mom whose adopted kids were in their teens. Geoff and Paula had two girls, ages eleven and fourteen.

His other perceptions were changing, too. How had he managed to drive down Safe Harbor Boulevard for a year without noticing either Krazy Kids Pizza or the Bear and Doll Boutique? This morning, their signs had jumped out at him. He suspected he'd be visiting those places with Dawn in the near future.

Since he really had consumed too much coffee—half a dozen cups by late afternoon—Edmond excused himself, cut through the outer office and passed Marie's desk. No clients waited in the small reception area—a far cry from the large law office where he'd worked as an associate. A few more years there and he'd have been in line to make partner, but in that high-pressure environment, what had once been a major life goal had loomed like a prison sentence.

The term *prison sentence* hit Edmond painfully. Today was Tuesday, which meant Barbara should be en route to the reception center in central California. He had a vision of his sister huddled in her seat, shaken by every jolt of the bus carrying her farther and farther from home.

He hadn't realized that Geoff had stepped into the room until he heard the man's soft voice say, "I won't ask if the situation's getting to you, because you wouldn't be human if it weren't. But since you've been standing here staring at the blinds for several minutes, why don't you take the rest of the afternoon off?"

Embarrassed, Edmond tilted his head in acknowledgment. "I *was* thinking about my sister, but I assure you, I'm on top of things."

"I never doubted it." Geoff Humphreys gave him a genial smile. Although only forty, the guy projected a fatherly air. His receding hairline and tendency to wear wrinkled suits wouldn't have stood him in good stead in L.A., but he had a gift for putting clients at ease. *And me,* Edmond conceded. "You don't have to maintain a stoic front, Edmond. If I can help, just ask."

"I could use some advice from your wife," Edmond said. "I hear she's a great teacher, and my niece will be entering second grade."

"Paula loves animals and uses them in her lessons because kids really respond to them," Geoff said. "She's even converted me, and I'm allergic to cats and was never keen on dogs. But now we have a houseful of pooches."

"That's great." The stray dog hairs on the man's suit were part of his down-home charm.

"Pets are great for kids, too," his boss added. "Your niece like them?"

"It's hardly fair to bring a pet into a home that's empty all day." Diplomatically, Edmond added, "Unlike yours, I'm sure."

"Don't worry. I'm not offended," Geoff said. "Besides, the dogs keep each other company. That's the trick. Don't stop at one."

"I'll remember that." *And run in the opposite direction.*

Edmond's cell phone sounded. As he answered, he gave Geoff a farewell nod and headed for his office.

It was Mark Rayburn. "Got a minute?"

"Sure."

"I'm hoping you can bail us out of a jam." The administrator's pleasant manner didn't hide the determined undercurrent of his words. "We have a lecture series here at the hospital called the Medical Insight Series. On Friday, a speaker from D.C. was scheduled to discuss changes in health care laws."

"Excellent topic." Through the window, Edmond noted a few cars traversing the narrow parking lot. The office's location in a strip mall might be far from glamorous, but the busy convenience store and dentist's office brought in foot traffic.

"Unfortunately, he's had to cancel." Frustration underscored Mark's tone. "I wondered if you'd be willing to step in."

That was a tall order. "Wouldn't Tony be more knowledgeable about changes in health care laws?" That wasn't Edmond's field, nor did he have time to research it this week.

"I didn't mean you had to address the same subject," Mark assured him. "How about new directions in family law? There *are* new directions in family law, aren't there?"

"Collaborative law," Edmond confirmed. "It's an area I'm focusing on more and more."

"Yes, I recall discussing it with you," the administrator said. "That would be fine."

"This is called the *Medical* Insight Series, though, not the Legal Insight Series," Edmond noted wryly. "Won't that topic disappoint the audience?"

"Just weave in a few case histories that relate to surrogacy and such," Mark replied. "After all, Safe Harbor specializes in family medical issues."

Preparing a speech would add to a heavy week's schedule. Still, Edmond appreciated the honor, and Geoff would be pleased at the publicity. "Sure. I'll be happy to step in."

"Thanks. I'm glad we can count on you."

Within minutes after the call ended, Edmond had already thought of several examples to enliven the talk. The prospect of headlining an event was invigorating, reminding him that he loved practicing law despite the pressure and the occasional frustration. Every day brought unique personalities and challenges that stimulated his mind and drew on his creativity. He enjoyed steering people through difficulties, analyzing their situations, mapping strategies and finding solutions.

Swiveling to his computer, Edmond opened a file and began jotting notes for his speech, energized for the first time in weeks.

Chapter Ten

Tuesday afternoon

Sender: Isabel Everhart
Subject: From Dawn

Hi, Uncle Eddie and Aunt Lissa,
Please rent the house with three bedrooms. Then Mommy can stay with us if she comes to visit. [From Isabel: I told her this can't happen, but she insists on including it.]

Grandpa helped me find the sports camp website. It says I can pick my favorite sports from a list. That will be fun.
XXX (kisses)
Dawn (and Isabel)

"Ask her what she likes to eat," Karen prompted as Melissa drafted a response on her laptop.

She paused with her fingers above the keys. "You really don't mind if they join us for dinner once in a while?"

"Are you kidding?" Karen sat beside her at the breakfast table, which doubled as a community desk in the evenings. Tonight, they had the house to themselves. Rod and Zora had gone to Jack's apartment to put away Anya's things. Lucky was out eating pizza and playing video games with his buddies. "Growing up, I wished for a houseful of brothers and sisters, plus cousins and aunts and uncles at the holidays. Heck, I'd have been grateful for a father who joined us for meals."

Karen's mentally ill father had rarely ventured down from the second floor, she'd explained to Melissa when they'd first become friends. He'd died when Karen was nineteen, more than twenty years ago. Her mother, a nurse, had supported the family, working until her sixties, when Parkinson's disease forced her to quit. Divorced from an abusive husband, Karen had moved in with her mother until the elder woman's death the previous December.

"You're about to get your wish for more people. It's going to be a full house soon." Melissa adjusted her bulge beneath the lip of the table. "Even fuller than usual."

"We should throw a baby shower for all three of you mommies." Karen loved organizing social events.

"Let's wait till the dust settles, okay?" They'd barely finished cleaning up after the wedding. "Besides, I'm borrowing so much stuff from our coworkers, I'm not sure what I lack."

"We should start a list."

Melissa groaned. "Not another list."

"I'll do it." Her friend tapped on her tablet computer to wake it up. "It'll be fun to coordinate. Even if we don't have a shower, your friends will want to buy gifts for you, and I'll make sure we don't duplicate stuff that you and Zora could share."

"Such as what?" With triplets, Melissa figured she'd be using everything from a changing table to high chairs practically nonstop.

"How many baby bathtubs will you and Zora use?" Karen responded.

"None for me. Too much trouble. My babies will have to be content with sponge baths." That gave Melissa an idea, though. "I'll bet there are lists of suggested baby gifts posted online. You could start with one of those."

Her friend checked in her tablet. "Found one! Ooh, it's long, and thorough." Karen scanned it. "Let's add a fund to hire Nanny Nancy."

"Who's Nanny Nancy?"

"A newborn care specialist who works with multiples." Karen was jotting notes as fast as her fingers could fly. "Several staffers at the hospital have used her. Don't forget, between you and Zora, we'll have five babies in the house. Too bad there isn't a spare room for a nursery."

"We could kick Lucky out," Melissa teased. She didn't mention Rod.

"I wouldn't do that to him." Her friend grew serious. "Although he may have to move if he can't find a job locally with his new administrative degree."

"One problem at a time."

"I'll post the list on my blog as soon as it's ready." Karen usually blogged about the pluses and minuses of sharing a house, without revealing too many personal details. "Don't forget, Anya's due in September. That's only a little over a month away."

"I can't think past Sunday." As she'd explained to Karen, Edmond was planning to collect Dawn that day. It was fortunate the girl had chosen the three-bedroom, which had already been vacated by its previous tenants and was ready for occupancy. The beach cottage wouldn't have been available for two weeks. "Speaking of which, I'd better finish my email to Dawn." Melissa and Edmond had agreed that their niece should hear from both of them.

Melissa and Edmond had only been married a year when Dawn was born, and she'd been surprised by the rush of love she'd experienced when she first held her niece in her arms. She and Edmond hadn't been around Barbara much during her pregnancy, due to Simon's hostility, but they'd been invited to the hospital.

The infant had gazed inquisitively up at her aunt, her little mouth working and her hands waving. Helpless, sweet, filled with potential, but starting off in difficult circumstances—Melissa had instantly sensed that their lives would forever be entwined.

Whatever fears she'd harbored about having a child of her own didn't apply to her niece. Being an aunt was pure pleasure. Over the next few years, they'd spent as much time together as Melissa and Edmond could manage, dropping in when Simon wasn't around or running into each other at family gatherings. But after the divorce, Barbara had become hard to reach, and Melissa had reluctantly eased off her relationship with Dawn. It felt like fate that she and Dawn were once again connected.

"Don't forget to ask about her favorite meals," Karen prompted.

"Okay." On her laptop, Melissa typed, What are your favorite foods? Maybe Isabel can send the recipes.

"I'm not sure if I should say anything about Barbara," she told Karen. "It bothers me that Dawn is hoping her mom can visit, as if she were away at college."

"The truth will sink in gradually." Despite being childless, Karen had excellent intuition. "Focus on the things she can look forward to."

"Us reading together. Fortunately, I'm well stocked." During the past few months, Melissa had bought picture books for her triplets, including the favorites she and Dawn had once shared.

Remember Goodnight Moon and The Runaway Bunny? she wrote. I'll bet you can read those aloud to me now that you're entering second grade. And the triplets can listen, too. Scientists say babies can hear while they're inside their mothers. Karen set down her tablet. "How about some hot cider?"

"That would be great." Even in midsummer, an ocean breeze cooled the house, especially at night.

While her friend bustled around the kitchen, Melissa closed her eyes, hearing the distant murmur of the ocean and the call of night birds from the estuary, her mind wandering to the conversation she'd had with Edmond last night and the mixed emotions she'd experienced. Observing how much he cared about Dawn had reawakened her belief that Edmond had a deep capacity for fatherhood. Yet people could only be pushed so far outside their comfort zone, and Edmond was already way past his.

Karen returned with two aromatic cups of cider enhanced by cinnamon sticks. Melissa inhaled with pleasure. "That smells fabulous."

"Netflix just posted new episodes of one of our favorite series," her friend said. "You in the mood?"

"You bet." After double-checking that she'd copied the email to Edmond, she hit Send.

Wednesday morning

Sender: Isabel Everhart
Subject: From Dawn

Hi, Uncle Eddie and Aunt Lissa,
My favorite food is peanut butter sandwiches with grape jelly. I love Grandma Isabel's fried chicken with peanut butter, too. It's supposed to be spicy but she takes the hot stuff out. I like bacon, freezer waffles and shredded-wheat cereal and orange juice. Artichokes are disgusting.

I'll read picture books to you and the babies. I'll sing to them, too. My favorite song is "The Wheels on the Bus."

Can I play with my new friends Tifany [Isabel: unsure of spelling] and Amber? They're nice.
Love,
Dawn (and Isabel)
Note from Isabel: As soon as I get a chance, I'll write down the chicken recipe and send it to you.

Wednesday afternoon

Sender: Edmond Everhart
Subject: We got the house!
Cc: Melissa Everhart

Dear Dawn and Isabel,
I signed a lease today for our house. I'll move my furniture in on Saturday, and I'll pick you up on Sunday afternoon, if that's okay.

Aunt Lissa will help me figure out what groceries and other items to buy. Also, don't forget I'll be there tomorrow (Thursday) at 5:30 for our 6 o'clock appointment with Dr. Brightman.

I enrolled you in sports camp starting Monday morning. I'll talk to Tiffany and Amber's parents about a playdate.
Love,
Uncle Eddie

Arriving "home" from work, Edmond slid his car into a parking space between a station wagon with an Arizona license plate and a hybrid sedan from Utah. The Harbor Suites rented rooms and one-bedroom apartments—furnished or unfurnished—by the day or week. During his yearlong stay, he'd noticed that many occupants or their relatives appeared to be undergoing treatment at the hospital.

When Edmond had moved in, he'd planned to find a better place within a few weeks. However, the rent was reasonable, with Wifi included, and what more did a guy need than a bedroom, living room and kitchenette? After he sporadically checked rental listings the first month, inertia had set in.

Walking between one-story buildings to his unit, Edmond had to admit he wouldn't miss the courtyard's squatty palm trees and nondescript shrubbery. Nevertheless, the prospect of renting an entire house and supervising a child elevated his stress level.

What was the big deal? he wondered as he unlocked the door of his apartment. He hadn't been nearly this uneasy about transitioning from a big L.A. law firm to Geoff's small office.

Inside, he flicked on the lights. At five-thirty the summer sky was still bright, but the unit had a gloomy air. He set his container of take-out pasta in the kitchenette for later and wedged his briefcase against the small table.

Melissa had texted that she was leaving the hospital shortly and would be stopping by on her way home. They'd agreed to split the shopping duties. Despite his aversion to cooking, Edmond was more comfortable buying groceries than towels and other household items, perhaps because he'd had to learn his way around a supermarket by necessity.

He hadn't realized how much he'd valued having a teammate at home. During their marriage, he and Melissa had divided responsibilities smoothly, both pitching in, planning little surprises, always homing in on exactly what the other person would enjoy. What a relief it was, knowing he could count on her.

Edmond went into the bathroom to clean his glasses and brush his hair. He contemplated changing into a fresh shirt, but decided not to risk getting caught half-dressed.

Returning to the front, he took a hard look at the room. When they'd divided the furniture, his wife had taken a love seat rather than the full-size couch and a white wrought-iron ice cream set over the bland kitchen table. It wasn't until he arrayed everything around his new apartment in L.A. that Edmond had been struck by the coldness of his impersonal furniture.

He'd believed it didn't matter, since he spent such long hours at work. The only thing he'd posted on the walls, there and here, was a photo montage from his and Melissa's trip to Italy. The happy memories the photos stirred outweighed the tinge of sadness he experienced about what he'd lost.

A tap at the entrance spurred Edmond into motion. When he opened the door, soft light haloed Melissa, highlighting the green and gold glints in her hazel eyes.

"Congratulations," she said.

"I'm sorry?" Standing close to her, he remembered that, in flat shoes, she only came up to his nose. In heels, she matched his five-feet-ten-inches.

"On the rental."

"Oh, right." He'd scored a victory in the housing market. "They received three applications. Luckily, your receptionist vouched for me with the landlord. Apparently her word carries weight."

"Caroline arranged for another renter a couple of years back, and that turned out well." Melissa stepped inside. "In fact, I was going to mention her. Harper Anthony, one of the nurses, has a daughter about a year older than Dawn and she's in sports camp, too. Harper's new husband Peter is the assistant director of the camp. Being a stepfather, he's sympathetic to kids in transition."

"I'll make a point of introducing myself. I presume the director will be there early." Sports camp opened its doors at 7 a.m. for the extended day program, which was convenient for working parents.

"Probably. Peter's very conscientious." Producing a pad and pen, Melissa prowled into the kitchen. "Shall we start in here?"

"Be my guest." Edmond opened one of the cabinets to reveal its limited contents. "I already have peanut butter, soup and canned vegetables."

"You should buy more of all. Also fresh fruit and vegetables." While jotting notes, she poked through the other cabinets and the fridge. "Stock up on nonperishables such as instant mashed potatoes, pasta and tomato sauce, and frozen meals. You're low on eggs and milk, too."

Edmond had had no idea how much food he'd need to stock in the house for him and Dawn, since as a bachelor he often grabbed a bite on his way to work or ate something from the vending machines. "I appreciate this. Dawn's list wasn't exactly comprehensive." The prospect of planning meals for the whole week intimidated him.

And not just one week. Week after week. Month after month, unless Barbara successfully appealed. He ran his hand through his hair, scarcely caring that he was mussing it.

"Take Dawn shopping with you next week. I'm sure she'll have ideas." Melissa's sensible suggestion restored his equilibrium. "I read on the website that sports camp includes a segment on nutrition. Still, you should buy her favorites to start, including bacon."

Bacon was one of the foods that Edmond ate only at restaurants. "What's the best way to fix it?"

"You can fry it in a pan or bake it in the oven," she said. "The internet's full of directions for cooking practically anything."

Ah, yes. "I'm good at searching."

"And you're a quick study."

"About some things." Edmond had soaked up information in school and he enjoyed exploring the law as it evolved. Cooking was another matter. When he'd been newly single, he'd learned the hard way that mistakes in cooking resulted in a pan full of charred ingredients.

As they proceeded through the apartment, the length of Melissa's second list surprised him. He'd figured he'd have to buy more towels, but hadn't considered a range of other items, including extra blankets, more pots, pans, flatware and kitchen utensils, and a stool to help Dawn reach higher shelves.

"After you're in the house, I'm sure there'll be additional shopping," Melissa advised.

"For what?" Edmond asked.

"Curtains, for one thing. As I recall, the blinds in that house provide privacy but they aren't decorative."

"Where does one buy curtains?" That was alien territory.

"Kitchens, Cooks and Linens sells ready-mades," she advised. "And don't forget gardening equipment. I'll bet Dawn will enjoy planting flowers."

"There are flowers there already." He'd noted a lively array near the front steps.

"Not in the backyard," Melissa said. "Then there's the lawn."

"The lawn," Edmond repeated in dismay. He hadn't mowed a lawn since his teen years.

"You can hire a gardener," Melissa assured him with a hint of a smile.

"Oh, right." While he'd considered the cost of child care, he hadn't factored in yard care. "And a cleaning service, too. Any recommendations?"

"We clean our own house, so I'm not sure. Just ask at work. You'll be inundated with suggestions." She was grinning widely.

"What's so funny?"

"You're usually on top of every situation." She slipped her pad into a pocket. "It's refreshing to see you out of your element."

"Refreshing?" That wasn't the word Edmond would have chosen. "Awkward, maybe. Embarrassing."

"No, it's cute." She'd never called him *that* before. "Human."

"As opposed to my usual robotic self?" he asked.

"In a sense," she teased. "It's fun to watch the ice melt."

He traced her temple with his thumb. "Only with you." Her radiance drew him in, drew him close. He tilted his head, longing for her, but holding back.

And then, as if it were the most natural thing in the world, she looped her arms around his shoulders and their mouths met. Edmond pulled her against him, shifting slightly to accommodate her midsection, and got lost in the joy of holding and treasuring this incredibly lovely woman.

Chapter Eleven

Edmond's spicy scent replenished Melissa's soul, while her body responded with a glorious ripple of desire. This was what home felt like.

She rubbed her cheek over the end-of-day stubble on his face, hardly daring to ease back enough to meet his gaze. When she did, she nearly got lost in the passion blazing from his eyes.

Breathing hard, he rubbed his chest over hers, arousing delicious sensations in her ultrasensitive breasts. Eagerly, Melissa angled her hips against him, and relished his hard response. Heat flashed through her.

His mouth claimed hers again, and they shifted through the bedroom door. Such a tidy room, yet infused with his male essence. Melissa unbuttoned his shirt, a shade of light blue with a pin-stripe, just like the ones she used to pick out for him.

Edmond caught her wrists gently to stop her. "Could this hurt you?"

"My doctor said it was okay at this stage unless there's bleeding." She hadn't thought she'd need to pursue any further information.

"I'd hate to cause you problems." His hoarse voice vibrated through her.

"It won't." She refused to stop now. Her usually guarded self had transformed into a driving force, fueled by three years of longing. No matter what issues divided them, Edmond had always been the standard against which she measured all men.

He nibbled her earlobe. With a sigh of surrender, Melissa buried her nose in his neck.

His hands caressed her as he unzipped her dress, a rose-colored maternity outfit she'd worn today to please him. But she'd never imagined this would happen.

When his hands cupped her bare breasts, Melissa gasped. "That's unbelievably intense."

"Does it hurt?" He paused, his eyes large and dark now that he'd removed his glasses.

"No, no."

"You're incredibly voluptuous." His gaze trailed down her nude, enlarged body.

"Does that mean coarse?" She'd been uncertain how the changes in her body might appear to him.

Edmond's palm stroked her stomach. "Just the opposite. It's as if you're complete, the way you were meant to be."

That was the sexiest thing he could have said. Melissa reached for the buckle on his pants. "Take those clothes off, mister."

"Yes, ma'am." Edmond grinned.

When they were both splendidly naked, they went to the bed. He yanked down the comforter and lowered her to the sheets. "Side, back, front, or some of each?" he teased.

"All of the above."

His long, lean frame fitted against her, each brush of his skin over hers arousing a cascade of sparks. Because of her size, front-to-front didn't work, so they shifted into a position they'd never before tried, his larger frame spooning hers from behind. When he entered her, a wave of joy carried her above her own body. Edmond's moan indicated his disbelieving pleasure.

Slowly, carefully, he probed her until excitement overwhelmed them and they thrust, writhed and clung to each other. Melissa lost track of her separateness, entangled with him in spirit as well as flesh.

They lingered in a state of bliss. After it ebbed, she nestled into him, wishing she could stay there forever. But unless Edmond's heart had room for three babies, that was impossible.

Gradually, she grew aware that it was getting late and she was hungry. She scooted up, her hair tumbling around her shoulders. "I'd better go."

Sitting beside her, Edmond kissed her temple. "I've missed you."

"Me, too." She ran her palms over his chest.

"Losing you cut me off from so many things. Even aspects of myself." His voice grew hoarse. "Melissa, what we had should have been enough. Why'd you have to throw it away?"

Her happy mood evaporated. "I'm not the one who threw it away, Eddie."

He raised his hands in a stop gesture. "Let's not get into that. I only meant—well, that our marriage was everything to me."

And to me...when we were younger. But she'd changed. Still, she'd have worked with him, delayed having children for a while and tried to find a way to satisfy both their needs, had he met her halfway. But much as she'd loved him, in the end, he hadn't been everything to her. "I wanted more," she said. "A family." A family that should have included him.

"I understand, or at least I'm trying to."

She moved to the side of the bed. "By the way, my housemates offered to help you move on Saturday. I can't do any lifting, but I'll bring the towels and stuff to your new place."

"Thank you," Edmond said. "For that, and for today."

Despite the pain he'd reawakened with his comment,

Melissa didn't regret making love with him. Tonight had been an unexpected gift from life. Even though he couldn't make room in his heart for her babies, she doubted she'd ever find anyone who aroused her this way. With the babies due and her own activities soon to be limited, their moments together were precious.

When she stood up, Edmond hurried around to lend a hand. In the bathroom, Melissa washed up quickly. Returning to the living room, she paused in front of the photo collage.

Earlier, she'd been too busy to spare it more than a passing glance. Now, she took in the scenes with enhanced emotion: a picture of her looking radiant that Edmond had shot in Pompeii; a romantic image of them against the Bay of Naples, snapped by a tour guide; a photo of Edmond gazing in awe at a jewel-like stained-glass window in a church on the Amalfi coast. She'd never have believed on that trip that their marriage wouldn't last.

"Do you ever wish we could go back and stay in Italy?" Edmond murmured beside her.

Sometimes. But that was her alternate life, and she'd chosen this one. "Since it's impossible, why worry about it?"

"Because we still mean something to each other," Edmond said. "But you're right."

After a brief hug, Melissa went out to her car. A part of her yearned to remain in Edmond's bed, curled against him until the rivers all ran dry. But then, in Southern California, the rivers ran dry every summer.

As she angled into the driver's seat, flurries in her abdomen reflected the babies' activity. Her daughters. Ironically, if Edmond had agreed to have a child three years ago, these babies would have been implanted in someone else. Yet she was convinced they were meant to be hers.

At her first meeting with Nell and Vern Grant, Melissa had experienced a strong sense of recognition. Although the two were a few years older than her and Edmond, their coloring and builds were similar. Nell, a kindergarten teacher, was more emotional than her husband, with a bubbly sense of humor. Vern, an accountant, appeared earnest and almost humorless, yet his loving glances at his wife reflected his devotion to her.

She'd followed their journey through *in vitro* more keenly than with most clients, sharing their heartbreak when the first attempt failed. After they'd undergone the stressful process of egg harvesting a second time, she'd rejoiced when they produced six viable embryos. What a miracle it had been when the first three implanted. Nell's pregnancy had flourished until she suffered a dangerous rise in blood pressure several weeks before her due date.

Mercifully, the babies—all boys—had been delivered safely by Caesarian section. Melissa had joined the parents in their hospital room—at their request—posing for photos with a baby in her arms while Vern cradled his other two sons.

As she held the little boy, a blond infant who could have passed for her son, tears had run down Melissa's cheeks. Overwhelmed by the ache for a baby of her own, she'd replaced the boy in his bassinet, invented an excuse and hurried off.

Nell must have noticed her emotions. In a vulnerable moment during the year-long fertility process, Melissa had confided to Nell the facts of her divorce and that she was considering artificial insemination.

Six weeks after the birth, the couple had concluded they couldn't risk a second pregnancy and would donate the surviving embryos. When they offered them to Melissa, Nell explained she'd had recurring dreams of Melissa as their mother. But the Grants had insisted that she decide quickly so they could settle the matter. If she delayed, they'd have chosen another recipient.

Now, she stared into the dusk beyond the windshield, revisiting her turbulent emotions as she'd weighed the unexpected proposal. Although Melissa had identified with the Grants and their babies, she knew these children might have been better off with a married couple.

But the chance to realize her dreams, especially given her bond with the Grants, had overridden her doubts. Although there'd been no specific agreement that she allow regular visits after the babies' birth, Melissa liked the idea that the families could remain in touch.

Ironically, once the initial excitement over the implantation faded, the Grants had been too overwhelmed caring for their triplets to keep up contact. In an email, Nell had noted that one little boy had required surgery to fix a newly discovered heart defect. Although he was doing well, she had no energy to spare.

Melissa's hand rested on her abdomen. Her body still vibrated with Edmond's lovemaking, yet these little girls weren't simply someone else's embryos. They were her daughters.

Despite the joy they'd shared today, despite the fact that she longed to share her future with a husband as well as her babies, she'd made the right choice.

THE COUNSELING CLINIC occupied a small white building on a busy street in the city of Garden Grove, midway between Norwalk and Safe Harbor. Edmond had chosen Franca Brightman, Ph.D., based on a recommendation from Paula Humphreys.

He'd brought Dawn for weekly sessions after Simon's death and Barbara's arrest, fearing that the events would traumatize his niece. Edmond had learned during his family law career that counseling could be vital. He'd seen fiercely antagonistic divorces defused by a counselor's insights into the couple's underlying issues.

His sister had consented to Dawn undergoing therapy, although she hadn't been thrilled. Resisting the possibility that she, too, might benefit, she'd only attended once, early in the process. That had relieved her concerns, although she'd still refused Edmond's offer to fund counseling for her, as well.

Initially, he'd believed that the point of therapy was to "fix" the child. But Franca had explained that the goal was to allow Dawn to integrate her experiences and gain the emotional tools to cope in the future. Edmond had wondered how such a thing was possible with a child her age— she'd only been six at the start—who would have trouble articulating her feelings.

Allowed to observe her first play therapy session, he'd tried not to be impatient, although the pace had seemed slow. Franca—she encouraged them both to use her first name—had allowed Dawn to choose among an array of toys and art supplies.

When the little girl began drawing, he'd expected the therapist to steer her toward depicting scenes that would reveal her inner landscape. Instead, Franca had simply observed, with occasional comments such as, "You enjoy using bright colors," or, "The way you sniff the crayons shows me that you enjoy the smell."

She wasn't praising or directing the little girl; instead, she was making Dawn aware of her own reactions. After several sessions, he'd found that his niece *was* better able to process her emotions and to communicate them.

Tonight, once Dawn went into Franca's office, Edmond sat alone in the waiting room. He no longer observed the play sessions, after Franca explained that Dawn should be free to interact with her away from him. Also, despite an impulse to keep close tabs on his niece, he didn't wish to control her. Mutual respect was important in their relationship.

Would a father—a worthwhile father, not a jerk like Simon—be so quick to loosen the reins? Edmond did care about Dawn, very much. Beyond that, he had to trust the therapist's recommendations and hope his instincts weren't seriously out of balance.

After checking his email on his phone, he glanced at the reading material arrayed on a low table in front of him. Choosing a parenting magazine, Edmond scanned an article about online safety, then flipped to a page about preparing for the start of school.

A photo of a woman with light hair, hazel eyes and a classic oval face reminded him of Melissa. Last night after she'd left, he'd slept still engulfed in emotions from their incredible lovemaking—regrets about their quarrel, a touch of anger that she'd pushed him away again. Confusion, too. Why couldn't he move past their relationship? Why was he still haunted by the sense that they belonged together?

After the divorce, he'd had one brief, unsatisfying relationship with a woman at his old law firm that had dissuaded Edmond from pursuing further affairs. He'd told himself he was waiting for the right woman. Making love to Melissa again had brought home the searing awareness that *she* was still the right woman. If only she'd waited before becoming pregnant, perhaps mothering Dawn would have satisfied her.

He didn't mean to resent those three little infants. And it was his own fault because he'd stupidly rushed to "solve" the situation.

The inner door opened. Dawn emerged, her little face more relaxed than when they'd arrived. "Franca wants you to go in."

He arose. "You're okay out here?"

"Yep. Don't forget to lock the door."

"Right." At the entrance, Edmond flipped the bolt, as he always did when leaving his niece alone in the waiting area.

As Dawn selected a picture book from the rack, he went inside. "Hi," he said to the slim, red-haired woman as she rose to greet him.

"Big changes this week." Franca, who could almost have passed for a teenager with her heart-shaped face and sprinkling of freckles, shook his hand firmly. "How're you holding up?"

He'd emailed her about Barbara's sentence and Dawn's planned move. He'd also sent her information about the social worker along with permission to provide input for the woman's report.

"My head's spinning," Edmond said as they sat in adult-size chairs. Surrounded by mostly tiny furniture, he felt like Gulliver among the Lilliputians.

"Dawn talked a lot about her Aunt Lissa. I presume that's your ex-wife." Earlier, he'd described the circumstances of his divorce to Franca. "She's expecting triplets?"

"That's right." Edmond set aside his instinct to keep personal matters private. That was counterproductive with a therapist. "It's an embryo adoption."

"That's unusual." While her calm manner revealed only nonjudgmental attentiveness, Edmond sensed there was a point to this discussion.

"She works in a fertility program in Safe Harbor Medical Center, where I'm consulting." He sketched their interaction over the past week, including the preparations for Dawn's arrival, but omitted their intimacy. That really *was* nobody's business. "Being around Melissa seems to be beneficial for my niece, especially since I have virtually no experience with parenting."

He expected the therapist to agree. Instead, she replied carefully, "It's understandable that you'd rely on her, since you have a friendly relationship with your ex-wife, and Dawn has a bond with her." As usual, Franca summarized complex matters succinctly. "But what happens after the triplets are born? Melinda—sorry, Melissa—will be up to her ears in babies. No matter how attached she is to Dawn, they'll have first claim on her."

"Well, of course." Because of the speed of the week's events, Edmond hadn't thought that far ahead.

"That will be another loss for Dawn, and imagine how she'll feel," Franca said earnestly. "She'll be devastated if she's counting on her aunt and is set aside for the babies."

Much as he wanted to deny that that might happen, Edmond couldn't. This pregnancy had to be Melissa's top consideration. "What do you propose?"

Franca spread her hands. "I'm not suggesting you break off contact with your ex-wife, only that she remain on the sidelines. You have to be the constant in Dawn's life. So spend time alone with her. Find activities you enjoy doing together. Other people may come and go, but it's vital that she's assured she can count on you, always."

Always. He nearly blurted that Barbara was still Dawn's parent and that hopefully she'd be out of prison in five years or less. But by then, Dawn would be nearly a teenager. Furthermore, Barbara would be an ex-con with no job. How long would it take Barb to reestablish her life, and at what point should he hand over his niece? She might stay with him until she was grown. Dawn deserved to be his first priority.

"Well?" The therapist watched him closely.

"You're right," Edmond said. "I'm Dawn's anchor." With those words, he sealed his commitment. No more hedging; no more considering this a temporary situation.

"This transitional period will involve a lot of ups and downs," Franca went on. "During what's called the honeymoon phase, your niece may strive to please you, to conform to whatever you ask. Once she's more confident, she'll test you by flouting the rules. When that happens, it may seem as if you're taking two steps backward for every step forward, but that's natural. She has to figure out where the boundaries are in her new landscape."

"And my job is to steer a steady course," Edmond said.

"Yes. Fortunately, you're up to the task." Her freckles stretched as she smiled.

"As I've explained, my plans didn't include fatherhood." He'd been open on that score. "But I understand my responsibilities, and Dawn's needs. I won't let her down."

"You may be pleasantly surprised to discover that parenting your niece is more rewarding than you expect," Franca said.

"I hope so."

As he rose to shake her hand, Edmond tried not to show how rattled he was at the prospect of distancing himself from Melissa. For Dawn's sake and in some ways his own, he couldn't entirely keep them apart. For starters, he'd promised to bring his niece to her house for Sunday dinner. And then there was his longing for Melissa, which defied reason.

You can handle this. As Franca said, you're up to the task.

In the waiting room, the little girl's face brightened when she saw him. And reaching for her hand, Edmond decided that finding things to do, just the two of them, might not be difficult after all.

Chapter Twelve

Sitting at the small desk in her bedroom, Melissa listened to Edmond in dismay. He'd called to explain the counselor's recommendation that she put distance between herself and Dawn.

"I love her," she protested.

"This isn't the end of your relationship," he assured her, his voice slightly rough at this hour. It was only nine-thirty, but no doubt he'd had a long day. "However, in your condition, you can't guarantee you'll be there for her when she needs you."

While Melissa assumed he was quoting the counselor accurately, she couldn't shake the suspicion he was deliberately pushing her away. "Are you angry at me?"

"About what?"

"We...sort of snapped at each other the other night." Surely he'd played their discussion through his mind as often as she'd played it through hers.

"No, I'm not angry," he said thoughtfully. "But, Melissa, even after all these years, we're both clearly still hurt and a little raw."

So he *was* pushing her away. "Are you going to change the plan to bring her over on Sunday night? I was just drafting an email to thank Isabel for sending the chicken recipe."

"No. She'll enjoy that, and so will I." His tone lightened. "And for what it's worth, Franca didn't say *I* had to avoid you."

If only he'd be clearer about what he meant! Melissa confined herself to a clipped response. "Well, I'll see you Friday, then."

"Friday?"

"At the hospital. I'm curious to hear your talk."

"Oh, yes. Great. Until then." On that note, the call ended. Frustrating man! Irritably, she reread the draft email.

Thursday night

Sender: Melissa Everhart
Subject: Thanks for the recipe
Cc: Edmond Everhart
Hi, Isabel and Dawn,
Isabel, thanks for the chicken recipe. My friend Karen plans to fix it for us Sunday night. Dawn, I can't wait to have you over! It'll be fun having you live so close. I'm sure we'll get together often.
Love,
Aunt Lissa

She'd have to revise it to sound more impersonal. Melissa blinked away tears—maternal hormones kept her emotions close to the surface these days.

Inside her, the babies were squiggling. Her palm traced the shape of her abdomen, which seemed to expand almost hourly.

When her daughters emerged into the world, they'd have only their mother to depend on. She would have to be all things to them, an intimidating prospect. Adding to her concern was the uncertainty about when they would arrive and whether there'd be complications. She supposed the counselor had a point.

All the same, she'd never shut out her niece. Quite the opposite—she longed to share her family-to-be with Edmond and Dawn.

For now, she'd have to retreat, but it hurt, both for her niece's sake and for Edmond's. The man deserved a slap to bring him to his senses. At the ridiculous image of herself punching out her ex-husband, Melissa laughed.

Then she rewrote the email, and hit Send.

Friday morning

Sender: Isabel Everhart
Subject: From Dawn
Cc: Edmond Everhart

Hi, Aunt Lissa,
    Grandma Isabel's been helping me pack. I can't wait until Sunday!
    Here are my favorite names for my little sisters [note from Isabel: that's how she refers to the triplets]. Bunny, Bambi and Belinda.
Love,
Dawn

On Friday afternoon, Edmond was pleasantly surprised to find the hospital auditorium nearly full for his talk. In view of the change of topic and speaker, he'd half expected attendance to be low.

Waiting on the side of the stage with public relations director Jennifer Serra Martin, he scanned the crowd. Immediately, he pinpointed Melissa between Karen and their supervisor, Jan Sargent. Meeting his gaze, his ex-wife nodded encouragement.

Although she'd accepted Franca Brightman's advice, he knew she was upset. He didn't like it, either. He and Melissa had been soul mates from the day they met, and it had torn him apart when they divorced.

Their lovemaking this week had shown how strong the bond remained, but it was no longer just the two of them. There was no question of bringing her three babies into his household, even if he'd been willing to consider it, because he couldn't risk letting his niece get lost in the shuffle. Dawn urgently required stability, reassurance and his full attention.

And, despite his best intentions, he still felt a twist of resentment about the pregnancy. If only she'd waited. If only she'd loved him as much as he'd loved her.

Edmond surveyed the rest of the attendees, recognizing a number of people including Vince Adams, who filled a center seat beside the administrator. Why was the gruff billionaire attending his talk?

Perhaps Mark had suggested it to further involve Vince with the hospital. The administration was hoping he'd give a major donation, as much as twenty million dollars, Tony had mentioned.

Adams, his wife and their daughters would be returning to their main residence in San Diego next month. They'd rented a beach cottage in Safe Harbor for the summer so the girls could be near their maternal grandmother, but school would be starting soon. And everyone in fund-raising knew that absence made the heart go wander.

"Let's get this show on the road," murmured Jennifer, a dark-haired woman with a throaty voice. Adjusting her note cards, she rose and approached the microphone. The audience chatter died.

"I'm Jennifer Martin, public relations director at Safe

Harbor Medical Center. Welcome to our latest Medical Insight lecture." Her formality reminded Edmond that the talk was being recorded and would be available on the hospital's website.

What he said and how he said it would affect many people's opinions of him, now and in the near future. It might also change a few lives. He couldn't wait.

MELISSA JOINED THE round of applause as Edmond took the mike. In a blue shirt, dark brown jacket and tan slacks, he struck a balance between professionalism and Southern California informality.

Following a few introductory remarks, he launched into his topic. "When I worked for a large law firm in L.A., I witnessed the ugly side of divorces, custody battles and cases involving adoptions and surrogacy. As many of you may have observed, nice people can become monsters when they feel as if their family is threatened. Sometimes the level of rage in those cases made me glad no one's invented a personal-size nuclear weapon."

A chuckle ran through the auditorium. Melissa's fists unclenched. She hadn't realized how tense she was on his behalf. During their marriage, she'd often experienced his emotions as if they were her own, a habit she'd picked up again, making it impossible to stop caring about him. If he didn't care about her, too, he shouldn't have moved to Safe Harbor. But then, he hadn't known about the triplets.

"Traditionally, for an attorney, handling divorces and custody cases means that your client either wins or loses. That's similar to criminal law, yet the overwhelming majority of our clients *aren't* criminals. I began to wonder why they, and we, acted as if they were."

The auditorium had fallen so quiet that a neighbor's sneeze startled Melissa. Everyone seemed mesmerized by Edmond's narrative.

"Over the past two decades, attorneys who share my aversion to these destructive processes have developed a field called collaborative law." He didn't bother to glance at the notes in his hand. Obviously, this was a subject he knew intimately.

"Collaborative law requires participants and attorneys to commit to the process of working together to seek reasonable solutions," he said. "We negotiate at group meetings, seeking to avoid going to court. The big savings in time and money appeal to many parties who initially resist the idea."

"What if all this collaboration stuff doesn't work?" The question, which Melissa considered rude since Edmond hadn't finished speaking, boomed from a man behind her. Swiveling, she recognized the speaker as Vince Adams, Tiffany and Amber's stepfather.

Privately, she doubted the billionaire would ever consider negotiating when his vast wealth allowed him to squash opponents through court battles, as he'd done with Rod Vintner over custody of the girls. She doubted that the youngsters' happiness had entered Vince's mind.

"Unfortunately, negotiations can fail, but we try to prevent that," Edmond responded. "Many collaborative law attorneys will not represent their clients should either side choose to litigate their dispute. The prospect of having to start over with new representation encourages clients to work harder for a solution. So does the awareness that they'll be running up a huge bill with no guarantee they'll get favorable results."

"Sounds good in theory, but it has to be damn hard in practice," Vince responded, as if this were a conversation between him and Edmond.

"It can be," Edmond agreed. "We have to educate clients that the desire to punish someone else is counterproductive. Breakthroughs occur when both parties are able to accord each other genuine respect."

He provided a few case histories of extended suits involving surrogacy and adoptions, with names and details changed to protect privacy, and compared these to cases where negotiations had brought about agreements.

"It's faster and more humane," he said. "And a lot easier on the attorney's nervous system."

Amid chuckles, Edmond opened the floor to further questions. Melissa admired how carefully he listened and how thoughtfully he responded. In several instances in which staffers appeared to be referring to a current situation, he offered to talk to them privately later.

The applause when he finished resounded in Melissa's ears. She swelled with pride.

In their own divorce, Edmond had behaved decently, dividing their assets down the line. Due to his higher income, he'd conceded to her attorney's demand for alimony, but that hadn't felt right to Melissa. While Edmond earned more, he'd also had law school debts and often sent money to his family. She'd inherited enough from her parents to pay off her student loans and tuck away a nest egg. So she'd declined the alimony, and had been rewarded by the gratitude in his eyes.

From an objective viewpoint, they'd behaved well. Internally, however, she'd been devastated. So, she was discovering, had he.

Why couldn't the man move past his rejection of fatherhood? He was doing so for his niece's sake. And while taking on three kids would be asking a lot, this man had far more internal resources than he realized.

The idiot needs to be part of a family. And so do I. But Melissa had no idea how to penetrate his bullheaded resistance. He'd have to discover the truth for himself. And that, she feared, might never happen.

Jennifer arose to thank the speaker and the audience. As the crowd dispersed, Edmond descended from the stage alongside the PR director. Melissa edged toward them to say a few words.

He was handing out business cards to a cluster of people, offering to meet with them during his office hours. Before she could move closer, Vince barreled into their midst, all but elbowing her and everyone else aside.

With Mark trailing apologies, everyone departed, including Melissa. Her congratulations could wait until tomorrow, and she didn't envy him having to talk to Vince.

EDMOND'S GUARD SHOT up as Vince approached, although he steeled himself to appear courteous. Fortunately, the interruptions during the talk hadn't thrown him off; lawyers had to be able to adjust their strategies quickly to challenges in a courtroom.

Furthermore, he had a favor to ask of Vince. Although to most men approving a children's playdate wouldn't qualify as a favor, he suspected that it might with Vince.

"I liked what you said about respect," Vince remarked in ringing tones as they shook hands. "Now if you can explain how to impress that on my wife, I'd be grateful."

What a personal thing to say, Edmond reflected, and how disrespectful of Portia Adams. "Is your wife here?"

"Oh, she's off with her mom and the kids, spending my money at the mall," the man responded. "I've had to commute from San Diego all summer because they miss Grandma. You see how I indulge her."

Edmond caught a meaningful glance from Mark. *Keep this guy happy* was the interpretation. "I'm sure she appreciates it."

"The hell she does." Vince didn't appear to care who overheard his remarks. Luckily the auditorium had emptied out. "You're probably aware, as the rest of the world is, that part of my interest in this hospital was to consult Dr. Rattigan about my infertility."

"How's it going?" Edmond didn't mean to pry, but Vince *had* raised the subject.

"The man's brilliant. The best in his field." At close range, Vince's breath carried a note of alcohol. While imbibing at lunch wasn't unusual, Edmond wondered if Vince was aware of how easily it had loosened his tongue. "He can't fix what's wrong with my sperm, but I could father a child using their high-tech magic—if my wife weren't so uptight."

"Maybe things can be worked out." Edmond deliberately kept his response vague.

"With all I've done for her, my wife refuses to undergo *in vitro*," Vince groused. "Doesn't want to take the hormones or some such thing. *I'm* willing to do whatever's necessary—a procedure that involves sticking a needle into my balls—but she's too finicky to do her share."

Despite a wince at the man's crudeness, Edmond maintained a bland expression. "That's too bad."

Actually, he didn't blame Portia. From what he'd learned, egg retrieval for fertilization in the lab required lengthy and stressful preparations that had serious potential side effects. Portia must be in her early forties, which meant carrying a child would also involve extra risks.

"What about a surrogate?" the administrator asked. "Anything you need is available here."

"I don't want a stranger involved, especially when my wife's presumably still fertile," Vince growled. "Now I wish I'd never started this business, consulting a men's fertility specialist. The word's spread that I'm less than a man. You have no idea what it's like, having people look down on you for being unable to father a child."

"Nobody looks down on you," Mark said.

"Yeah? I can sense how the staff reacts when they think I don't notice." Vince appeared to be building up a head of steam. "It's time I took my toys and went home."

Alarm flashed across the administrator's face. Although Edmond hated to cater to this egotistical man just for the sake of a donation, there was a lot riding on the proposed expansion. Mark had explained that the hospital hoped to convert a nearby former dental building to provide not only labs and treatment facilities for the men's program but also office space for a wide range of doctors. It would mean some of them, including Jack, would no longer have to work odd hours in shared quarters. And Melissa's house-mate Lucky might be able to use his newly minted administrative degree here at home.

"I do understand some of what you're experiencing, although it's my own doing." In the interest of male bonding, Edmond forced himself to overcome his repugnance at sharing personal details. "I got a vasectomy without considering all the consequences."

"Such as?"

Might as well tell the whole story. "My wife left me."

"Ever consider reversing it?" Vince asked, his interest piqued.

"Not really, although if I had it to do over..." Edmond couldn't finish the sentence, because he wasn't sure how it ended. Instead, he said, "In any event, I have other priorities at the moment. I have to take guardianship of my niece, the little girl who was with me at the wedding."

"How come?"

"Dawn's father is dead and her mom, my sister, is dealing with her own issues." That provided a chance to bring up Dawn's request. "By the way, your daughters were a hit with her. It would be great if they could play together before school starts."

"So that's who the girls were chattering about—Dawn, you say?"

"That's her."

Vince produced a card. "Here's my cell number. Sure, let's set it up."

Edmond reciprocated with his own card. "I'm in learning mode when it comes to parenting. Any tips you can provide would be welcome." Not that he seriously expected Vince to have worthwhile insights, but even a stopped clock was right twice a day.

"Here's my advice. Don't let them get the bit between their teeth or they'll run you ragged," the man boomed.

"I'll remember that."

Vince beamed in satisfaction. "The hospital made a smart move when they hired you. You're my kind of guy."

Edmond couldn't honestly return the compliment. Instead, he ventured, "Don't give up on fatherhood yet. Your wife might change her mind."

"I suppose so. With Dr. Rattigan right here, this is too great an opportunity to pass up," Vince agreed.

"Maybe we can take the girls to the Bear and Doll Boutique in town," Edmond suggested. "I understand they offer children's craft classes." Geoff Humphreys had suggested the trip, since his mother owned the shop.

"I'll let you sort that out with my wife," Vince said.

On that note, they shook hands, and Vince departed with the administrator. Edmond debated stopping by Melissa's office, but it was after five o'clock and he had to finish preparing for tomorrow's move.

As he reached his car in the parking structure, his cell rang. It was Mark. "Thank you for bringing Vince down from the ledge," the administrator said. "You're a born diplomat."

"I was planning to ask him about the playdate anyway." Edmond didn't want to leave the impression that he enjoyed cozying up to donors.

"Well, he stopped talking about leaving for San Diego right away," the administrator told him. "Hopefully we're on track again, especially after I reminded him that the program and the building would bear his name."

"I'm glad I could help."

This had been a productive afternoon, Edmond reflected after the call ended. Scoring a success in his consulting job helped restore his sense of balance, which had been shaky since Monday's sentencing.

He'd been drawn to the law because of its logic, its order, its appeal to the rational. Edmond was most comfortable when employing his intellect, and most like a fish out of water when relying on his instincts.

That was Melissa's specialty. Facing the next few weeks without relying on her was a daunting prospect, especially since this weekend marked Edmond's transition into being Dawn's full-time guardian. Maybe he'd ask her for some last-minute tips....

Chapter Thirteen

You're officially out of your mind. Ruefully, Melissa watched Edmond sleep in the morning light, his body sprawled across the bed, his tousled hair and bare torso tempting her to rouse him for another round of lovemaking. She should be more restrained, she supposed, but in view of her pregnancy and the fact that Dawn was moving in today, this might be their last such encounter.

Yesterday, while she'd folded the new linens and organized the kitchen, Lucky, Rod and Jack—back from his honeymoon and relieved to find Anya's belongings already in the apartment—had hauled Edmond's modest furnishings in his rented van to his new home.

She and Edmond had required only a glance or a few words to decide which item belonged in which room and how to orient the larger pieces of furniture. They shared an aesthetic about such matters.

After the others left, he'd invited Melissa to stay and share takeout. He'd seemed more open and vulnerable than usual, and it had occurred to her that he might be ready to begin a shift in his views about family. To be honest, she'd also craved this last chance to be close to him.

After dinner, they'd watched a documentary about the rapid expansion of Shanghai, one of the cities they'd visited during their marriage. Memories had surged of viewing the city's impressive museum, enjoying a river cruise at sunset and touring the waterfront Bund area with its colonial-era buildings. How carefree they'd been.

She had no excuses for sliding on his lap and enjoying his caresses save that she wanted to be that lighthearted just once more. With Edmond, she wasn't just a mother and a counselor, she was also a woman. And there was only one man who'd ever made her feel like one.

But she was putting her heart at risk, and for what? Dreams that refused to come true.

Beside Melissa, Edmond stretched and let out a groan. "I'm stiff as a—is there anything stiffer than a board?"

"An iron rod, although you already have one of those," she teased.

He laughed. "I'm afraid it may not live up to its reputation right now. Any chance of a massage?"

"I can try." Leveraging herself to sit on his back, Melissa kneaded the muscles along Edmond's spine and shoulders. Gradually, his knots dissolved beneath the pressure. He'd kept his body in excellent shape, she noted appreciatively, and his skin was smooth.

"You're next." Lazily, he helped her lie on her side. One leg resting lightly atop her thigh, he massaged her from behind, sending tingles of pleasure along her nerve endings. His hands hadn't lost their expertise in probing exactly the right points.

When he finished, they lay spooning, one of his palms cupping her abdomen. She scarcely noticed the ripple, but he gave a start. "What's that?"

Melissa sighed. "My girls are playing kickball."

"Does it hurt?"

"No. It tickles a little, though," she admitted.

His hand, which had jerked away, rested on her belly again, the heat soothing into her. "Can they feel it when I touch you?" he asked.

"I doubt it. But they can hear your voice."

"How about this?" Putting his mouth to her stomach, he blew on it, creating a raucous noise.

Chuckling as she pushed him away, Melissa retorted, "That tickles even more!"

"You said they were playing." His eyes widened in mock innocence.

Could he be changing, viewing these little ones as children instead of a burden? Melissa knew better than to push the issue, though.

"Just wait till they're crawling all over the carpet. Remember how destructive Dawn was when she was little?" What a cutie their niece had been, Melissa recalled. "They'll be grabbing things and climbing in our laps and sticking stuff in their mouths."

"Speaking of putting things in our mouths, how about a cheese Danish?" he asked. "On Sunday mornings, nutrition doesn't count."

"Yes, it does, but I'll make an exception."

They ate in the kitchen, reading the advance edition of the newspaper they'd bought last night. It might not have the morning news, but all the inside sections were there.

Resting her feet on Edmond's thighs beneath the table, Melissa reflected that all Sundays should be so companionable and peaceful. Yet before too long, her daughters would be old enough to enjoy the comics with them.

With me, she corrected sadly, and barely restrained the urge to kick him.

Time to go. Although she'd have liked to greet Dawn here at her new home, Melissa didn't intend to press for that. Also, the pair would be joining her household for dinner tonight.

And maybe talking about the triplets had planted a seed in Edmond's fertile brain. At the image, she had to hide a smile.

She wasn't ready to give up on him. Even if that did make her the world's biggest numbskull.

"Are Tiffany and Amber here?" Dawn's wide-eyed gaze met Melissa's as she opened the door to welcome her niece and Edmond for dinner.

"I'm afraid nothing's been arranged yet." Heavens, the child had only moved into her new home today, and already she was eager for a playdate. "Your uncle's working on it."

"I sent their parents an email Friday night." Edmond, his brown hair still damp from the shower, ushered the little girl inside. He'd obviously cleaned up after the move.

Melissa transferred her attention to Dawn, who wore a crisp pink dress and a fresh ribbon in her bouncy brown curls. "My, you look pretty."

A pucker formed between Dawn's eyebrows as she peered into the living room. "Where did the chairs go?"

"We were only renting them for the wedding." Melissa closed the door behind her guests. "It's nice to have the couch in its proper place."

Dawn sighed. "I miss the flowers."

"So do I," Melissa agreed.

"Something smells wonderful." Edmond inhaled for emphasis. "Very spicy. Though I'd hoped Karen would wait to show me how to fix the chicken."

"She had to marinate it for a few hours," she explained.

"It has to marinate?" He ducked his head. "This is more complicated than I expected."

"It's worth it," Dawn told him.

"I'm sure it is." He gave her shoulder a pat. "Your uncle's a beginner chef. *Very* beginner."

"That's okay," his niece said earnestly. "We all have to start somewhere."

He gave a startled laugh, and Melissa grinned. "You're right, Dawn."

"She often is," he said, flexing his shoulders. He must be sore; Melissa's mind flashed to their erotic massage.

"I want to visit your room, Aunt Lissa." Dawn said.

Edmond's eyes narrowed, but since they hadn't broken the news to Dawn that her aunt was supposed to keep a distance, what reason could they give? "Sure."

"I'll try to learn something in the kitchen," Edmond said. "Dawn, don't stay up there too long. You're the expert on peanut-butter chicken and we may need your advice."

"I have to read Aunt Lissa the letter Mommy wrote." From her small patent-leather purse, Dawn retrieved a wrinkled sheet of paper.

"You heard from Barbara?" This must have been a relief to Dawn. "How is she?"

"The letter arrived at my parents' house yesterday." Edmond explained. "She seems in upbeat spirits, considering." Or she'd tried to appear that way for her daughter's sake, Melissa gathered.

"Don't tell her what it says!" Taking her aunt's hand, Dawn tugged her toward the stairs. "I'll read it to the babies, too."

"I'm sure they'll like that." *And so will I.*

WHILE KAREN SHOWED Edmond how to dredge the marinated chicken in flour and fry batches of it in oil, Lucky chopped vegetables from the garden. He had a large pile, including carrots, onions, zucchini, green beans, tomatoes, yellow squash and assorted greens.

"I'll stir-fry these with tofu, since I'm a vegetarian," the male nurse explained when Edmond asked what he was preparing.

"Zora fixed a salad earlier," Karen added, repositioning the clip that held her reddish-brown hair out of her face.

"Where's Rod?" Edmond missed the colorful anesthesiologist, who'd provided humorous commentary during yesterday's move, although he hadn't done much heavy lifting.

"He took Jack and Anya out for dinner," Lucky said. "There's just five of us tonight."

"Oh, is that all?" Edmond murmured.

Karen laughed. "The house feels empty without a crowd. I appreciate you and your niece joining us."

"I can't tell you how great this is for us." With Isabel's input, he'd planned a week's worth of meals. Preparing them still loomed as a major challenge.

While the chicken was frying, Karen carried dishes into the dining room to set the table. Edmond assisted Lucky at a second cutting board. "There sure is a lot of chopping involved, not that I'm complaining."

"That's the fun part about cooking vegetables." The man's knife flew, dicing a white globe that might be a turnip. "You can start with a basic sauce, such as sweet and sour, and throw in whatever's handy. If you have a couple of this and a few of that, it all goes into the dish."

Karen returned for silverware. "Did I hear you say earlier that you're arranging a get-together with the Adams girls?"

"Dawn asked to play with her friends again," Edmond confirmed. "I was planning on taking them to a workshop to learn how to sew doll clothes."

"Sounds fun," she said.

"To you maybe," Lucky muttered.

"How does this playdate thing work, anyway?" Edmond asked. "Do the parents stick around?"

"Depends on the activity, I presume," she said. "Since I don't have kids, my knowledge is theoretical."

Lucky handed Edmond several large tomatoes. "Don't chop these too small. Quarters will be fine."

"Start by inserting the point of the knife," Karen warned.

"If you slice straight down and the knife isn't super-sharp, you might use too much pressure. Then, squish."

Edmond glanced at the red splotch blossoming on his apron. "Too late."

"You'll live," she assessed, and walked back into the dining room.

Following her directions, he did a neater job with the rest of the tomatoes. Then he started in on a carrot. *That* wouldn't squirt him.

"Rather than sewing classes, why not volunteer at the animal shelter?" Lucky said. "More fun for everyone, and you might do some good."

"I'll look into it." The prospect of cleaning cages didn't thrill Edmond. Still, he wasn't eager to spend an afternoon hunched over a table in a doll shop, either.

"Word of warning," Karen interjected as she reentered. "Rod volunteers at the shelter on Saturday afternoons. Running into him could be awkward."

"He should stay home that day." Lucky had no hesitation about ordering people around, Edmond mused.

"Surely it isn't that terrible if he runs into his daughters," he said.

"Vince has threatened to slap him with an injunction." Karen scowled. "I try not to hate that man, but it's hard."

"I have to admit, I'm torn, too." Lucky set his pot of vegetables on the stove. "An expansion of the men's fertility program could mean a lot to my career. And it'd be a good thing for our patients," he added. "But the guy's a creep."

"It's too bad." Rod obviously loved his daughters, regardless of not being related to them genetically. *Just as Melissa loves her babies.* Edmond had grown up hearing the philosophy that blood was thicker than water. Technically, that might be true, but now he was viewing relationships in a different light.

Dawn and Melissa appeared. "I'm hungry," the little girl announced. "Aren't you hungry, Aunt Lissa?"

"Pregnant women are always hungry," Melissa said.

"That's 'cause you're feeding the babies." Beaming, Dawn patted her aunt's belly.

"The chicken's done." With tongs, Karen transferred the pieces to a plate. "Would somebody please call Zora?"

"Zora!" Dawn yelled.

Everybody laughed. Edmond made a mental note that kids tended to take things literally. Or maybe his niece was joking. She had all sorts of hidden qualities, he was happily discovering.

EVERYONE DUG INTO the meal with enthusiasm. Flavored with allspice and cayenne as well as buttermilk and peanut butter, the chicken proved delicious. The prep time had been rather long, in Melissa's view, but this was a special occasion.

Overexcited by the day's events, Dawn ate only a few mouthfuls before plying Zora with questions about her twins. In short order, the little girl learned that they were a girl and a boy, that Zora hadn't selected names yet and that the father was her ex-husband.

"You used to be married like Uncle Eddie and Aunt Lissa?" Dawn asked.

"Kind of." Zora shifted uncomfortably.

"Has *he* picked out names?" the little girl pressed.

"He doesn't know he's going to be a daddy," Zora said.

"Not all former spouses get along as well as Uncle Eddie and I do," Melissa advised.

"Also, your uncle's a decent chap who takes care of his family," Lucky put in. "Whereas Andrew..."

"Lay off him, would you?" In her prickly mood, Zora's short ginger hair gave her an electrified appearance.

"I should expect you'd be heaping insults on him, considering how he's treated you," Lucky said.

"That's my decision," Zora answered.

Melissa toyed with her fork, reluctant to interfere yet unhappy that the pair were sniping. For some reason, Lucky seemed to take Zora's situation personally, although neither of them showed any romantic inclination toward the other.

"As long as your attorney's here, why not ask him about notifying Andrew that you're pregnant?" Lucky persisted. "I'll bet the father has a legal right to be informed."

"Does he?" Zora addressed Edmond.

He finished a mouthful of Lucky's tofu dish. "When the baby's born, you'll be asked to identify the father for the birth records."

"But then Betsy will find out, and she'll tell him," Zora protested.

Dawn listened wide-eyed. "Who's Betsy?"

"Andrew's mother," Lucky said. "She's the nursing supervisor at the hospital. And if you ask me, a grandmother has a right to know, too."

Karen clinked her spoon against her plate. "Lucky, Zora's told you to stay out of it. Being her housemate doesn't give you big-brother privileges."

"Someone has to put her straight," Lucky grumped. "Otherwise she'll go right on making one bad choice after another."

"Like my mommy," Dawn said. "That's why she's in prison. She says so in her letter."

Zora, who'd opened her mouth to reply, turned her attention to the little girl. "I'm sorry your mom's in trouble. But Lucky has no right to compare my situation to criminal activity."

"I didn't," he protested.

Karen slapped the table, rattling the dishes. "Enough!"

To distract her niece, Melissa said. "Dawn, you've hardly tasted your chicken."

The little girl heaved a melodramatic sigh. "Why do grown-ups always stop talking at the most interesting parts?"

Melissa wished she had an answer. No one else did, either, until Edmond spoke.

"As grown-ups, we should be mature enough to solve our problems without fighting." He traced a finger over his niece's temple, brushing away a curl that had drifted close to her mouth. "We should show children the right way to work out differences, which is to be kind and respectful."

"That's not how people act on TV," she protested. "They do mean things to each other."

"Which is an excellent argument for avoiding the boob tube," Lucky said.

Dawn giggled. "The boob tube! That's funny."

"TVs used to have an actual tube inside, called a cathode ray tube," Edmond informed his niece. "That might be where the term comes from."

"What's inside them now?" Dawn popped a forkful of salad in her mouth.

"Something called a liquid crystal display," Lucky said. "I won't go into the tedious details, mostly because I'd have to research them."

From there, the conversation veered to speculation about the upcoming fall TV season. Her eyes glazing over, Dawn focused on her meal.

Melissa wasn't sure boring a child was the best way to avoid ticklish topics. For the moment, however, a whole tableful of adults had no better idea. How was Edmond going to manage parenting on his own?

THE ALARM WOKE Edmond an hour early Monday morning. He'd set it early so he had extra time to introduce Dawn to sports camp. Even though he'd signed her up online, he wasn't about to drop off a seven-year-old without a close look at the situation. Also, afterward he had to prepare for his office hours at the hospital, with several consultations scheduled as a result of Friday's talk.

Blinking his eyes open in the unfamiliar light of his new bedroom, he switched off the alarm and stretched. Ouch. His muscles ached in places he hadn't been aware of since he'd done construction in college.

Too bad Melissa wasn't here to massage him. And kiss him. And… But they'd both understood that couldn't continue. Still, this wasn't a bad way to start the week, swinging out of bed to the tantalizing scents of bacon frying and coffee brewing.

Wait a minute. Who was cooking breakfast?

The last trace of sleepiness vanished as Edmond leaped to his feet, pulled a bathrobe over his pajamas and raced down the hall.

Chapter Fourteen

Dressed in jeans and a T-shirt, Dawn stood on a stool by the stove, flipping bacon over with a fork. The frying pan sizzled and spattered. Nearby, slices of bread had emerged nicely browned from the toaster, while a full pot of coffee hissed as the last few drops fell into it from the coffeemaker.

Edmond's urge to yell "Stop!" faded as he caught his niece's proud smile and heard her cheerful greeting. "Good morning, Uncle Eddie!"

"Good morning, cutie." He debated whether to order her away from the stove before she burned herself. However, he hated to spoil her happy mood. Also, since he had no experience in frying bacon, his fumbling might only emphasize that she'd been right to take charge. "Thank you for fixing breakfast."

"It was fun. You bought my favorite stuff." After switching off the burner, she lifted slices of bacon and set them atop paper towels. "I love bacon!"

"Me, too." Still debating how to approach the topic of safety, Edmond took out plates and napkins, along with flatware.

"There's coffee." Dawn regarded him expectantly, waiting for a compliment.

"You're a talented little girl." He poured himself a cup. "You don't...do you drink this stuff?"

Her nose wrinkled. "Ugh."

Thank goodness. There was one bad habit he didn't have to break her of. After taking a sip, Edmond said, "This is great."

"Daddy showed me how to make it nice and strong." Dawn fetched a tub of margarine from the refrigerator along with a carton of juice.

After opening a jar of orange marmalade, Edmond sat at the table across from her. "Did you cook for your parents every morning?"

"Only when they were over hung," she said.

"Hungover?" The revelation chilled him. "Both your mommy and your daddy?"

Nodding, she spread marmalade on her toast. "This smells like oranges. I never had it before."

"I like it better than grape jelly."

She took a bite. "Me, too." .

Edmond ate in silence for a while, processing what he'd learned. He'd always assumed that his sister, for all her faults, took decent care of her daughter. Instead, he'd just learned that Barbara had drunk to excess and allowed her little girl to risk serious burns. Simon had actually instructed Dawn in brewing coffee so the child could cater to him, instead of being concerned about *her* well-being. And his sister had allowed that, too.

With a jolt, he reflected that if Barbara did appeal and gained release, he wasn't about to relinquish Dawn without making absolutely certain she'd have proper supervision. If his sister sought to reclaim her daughter, he'd be even tougher on her than child protective services would be.

To his niece, he said, "You're a wonderful little girl and I appreciate this breakfast."

Dawn's forehead creased with worry. Clearly she'd detected a "but" fast approaching.

"From now on, it's fine for you to get out cereal, bread, milk and juice, but please don't use the stove or the oven when I'm not around," he said. "If you want to set up the coffee, that's okay, but don't turn it on."

Her mouth trembled. "Why?"

Edmond hadn't meant to upset her. "You didn't do anything wrong. But even though you're a good cook, you might get burned, and it's my job to protect you." Another point occurred to him. "No using sharp knives unless I'm around, either."

"That's silly." Her mouth clamped shut, as if she were afraid to say more.

"You can still cook when I'm with you."

"What about when you're sleeping?" she demanded.

Clearly, his point hadn't sunk in. What did parents do in such a situation? Simply ordering her to obey might backfire.

In persuading a jury, he'd learned that people responded best when explanations made sense to them. "Here's the thing," Edmond told his niece. "Family services has to make sure I'm a fit guardian for you. If they find out I'm letting you do something they consider dangerous, I could get in trouble."

"Will they take me away?" Tears glimmered in her eyes.

"That's not likely," Edmond said. "But it's important that we follow the rules. You won't always know what those are, so if I correct you, please don't assume I'm angry."

"You're not mad at me?"

"Oh, honey, no."

When she scooted onto his lap, Edmond hugged the little girl, and discovered his eyes were wet.

In his ear, she murmured, "Can I still use the toaster?"

Edmond laughed. "You bet. Just keep a close eye on it. And thank you again for breakfast."

Maybe he wasn't so bad at this guardian thing after all.

THE SHOUTS OF children and coaches rang through the community college gymnasium as Edmond walked in. Dawn, marching beside him with her backpack, grabbed his hand and hung on tight.

Around him milled parents with their kids, who ranged from preschoolers up through sixth graders. Edmond noted banners designating which age groups were to gather in what parts of the gym. College-age counselors in red T-shirts cheerfully directed kids, as well.

The website said the camp had been established both to keep kids active during the summer and to train college students who planned to work in physical education. Parents seemed willing to trust their kids to these youngsters and depart, but Edmond gazed around until he spotted a man of about thirty in a black T-shirt bearing the red-lettered words *Head Honcho*. Roughly Edmond's height, the man had the build of a wrestler. He must be Peter Gladstone, the director.

According to Melissa, Peter was a high school biology teacher during the school year. His wife, a nurse, had previously rented the house Edmond and Dawn now occupied. Safe Harbor was definitely a small town, he mused as they approached Peter.

"Mr. Gladstone? Edmond Everhart." He thrust out his hand, which Peter grasped firmly. "This is Dawn."

"Hello, young lady." Peter reached to shake her hand, too, but Dawn scurried behind Edmond. "This place can be scary, can't it? It's loud, too."

Her head bobbed.

He waved over a girl with a snub nose and honey-brown hair. "My stepdaughter will explain to Dawn how things work. Mia turned eight a few weeks ago, so she's in the next older group, but she's a sports camp veteran."

"Hi!" Mia gave Dawn a high-five. "My Mom told me about you. We used to live in your house. I have a black-and-white kitty named Po. Do you have any pets?"

"No."

"Come on, I'll show you where you're s'posed to be." Mia linked her arm through Dawn's. "I have two baby brothers. A surrogate mommy gave birth to them last month. Their names are Jacob and Jason."

"I'm going to have three baby sisters," Dawn said. "They don't have names yet."

Mia whisked Dawn away before Edmond could correct that the triplets weren't her sisters. Besides, he had a more pressing question, in view of the number of people milling around and the openness of the facility. "How do you maintain security?" he asked Peter.

"We check off each child's whereabouts repeatedly throughout the day." Peter showed him the tablet computer where he kept track. "Visitors are strictly monitored." He indicated the badge Edmond had received when he signed in at the door. "You're welcome to stop by at any time. Things appear hectic right now, but it's quite different once the kids split into separate activities and the parents go home or to work."

Reassured, Edmond yielded when another parent broke in with a question. This seemed as safe a locale as any for his niece.

Preparing to leave, he spotted Dawn standing with Mia near the bleachers under a banner reading K-2. Kindergarten through second grade, Edmond translated mentally. Soon the jargon would become second nature, no doubt.

The two girls were talking animatedly. When Edmond waved, Dawn waved back almost perfunctorily.

Already she was making friends, Edmond thought as he wove his way through arriving parents and campers. Funny thing was, he had a twinge of disappointment at being so readily displaced.

Maybe that was how real parents felt, too.

EDMOND ARRIVED AT the hospital half an hour early for his first appointment and decided to stop by Melissa's office.

If she was busy, he could leave, but he found he wanted to tell her everything that had happened since she'd left the other day.

Edmond walked down the hallway to the fertility program offices. He'd expected to pop in to see Melissa unobserved, but he hadn't reckoned on the eagle eye of the receptionist.

"Hey there!" Caroline Carter swung around from a file cabinet, setting a manila folder atop the open drawer. "How do you like the house?"

Since she'd recommended it and provided a referral to the landlord, she deserved more than a superficial answer. "Lovely. A bit cavernous until I buy more furniture, but it's nice not bumping into the walls every few steps."

"Is Dawn enjoying sports camp?" she asked. "I'll bet Mia showed her the ropes. She's a little sweetheart."

Did the woman track everything? Edmond didn't mind, considering how helpful she was.

"Dawn and Mia have become fast friends, and Peter Gladstone's a nice guy." Since Melissa had just appeared in the doorway of her office, Edmond addressed his summary to her, as well.

"That reminds me, the Gladstones write children's books about backyard biology," Caroline said. "I brought you one."

"That's very kind of you." Edmond was impressed by her generosity. "You didn't have to do that."

"I ordered a whole stack," Caroline said. "I'm proud to know the authors."

"Harper takes the photos and Peter writes the text," Melissa added.

"Where do they find the energy?" As Edmond recalled, the couple had one little girl, two babies and two jobs.

"I doubt they've done any writing since the twins were born." From a desk drawer, Caroline handed him a book with a stunning cover photo of a butterfly. "It explains how to identify insects in your yard. Mia added her photos and comments, too."

"That little girl's an author?" Leafing through it, Edmond was impressed with the quality of the pictures and the easy-to-read layout and text. "They've done an impressive job. Thank you, Caroline."

"Enjoy!"

"Many of those were shot in your yard," Melissa noted as he followed her into her office. "Dawn should love that."

"I love it, too." He looked forward to sharing the book with his niece.

"Things went well this morning?" Melissa closed the door behind them.

"Sports camp, yes. However, we did run into a rough patch earlier." He described the cooking incident and how he'd handled it.

"That was wise." As she sat in her chair, Melissa rubbed her belly. Forestalling his question, she explained, "Just some stretching pains in my abdomen. I have a doctor's appointment today. I'm hoping I won't have to limit my activities for another few weeks."

Concern jolted through him. How frustrating that, just when the risks from her pregnancy were increasing, his obligations to Dawn limited his ability to assist her. Now he might not even see her at work, and, to be honest, he'd come to rely on her as a friend and a sounding board. "Let me know what I can do."

"I will." She folded her hands on the desk. "Now, let's hear about sports camp. How's Dawn taking it?"

He sketched the experience, drawing a smile as he described the girls' busy chatter. "Mia seems very secure, considering the changes in her life."

"Yes, she does."

His thoughts turned to the twins. "Do the Gladstones

leave their babies in the hospital child center while they work?" He presumed Melissa would do the same with her triplets.

"Harper's on leave," she said. "Twins are a challenge, even for an experienced mom, although not having to recover from a pregnancy makes things easier, I'm sure."

What about you? He wondered how she as a single mother could cope with so many babies alone.

Melissa always seemed organized and in control, the person that everyone else depended on. Only once during their marriage had she fallen apart, after her parents' deaths, crying in his arms and admitting she felt overwhelmed by the details of arranging funerals and settling their estates.

Edmond had been grateful for the chance to comfort her and take on some of her burdens. Then, just as she was recovering from her grief, his own mother had died, and Melissa had slipped into support mode.

He certainly didn't wish for her to fall apart again. But he hoped she'd lean on him if she needed to.

Her next question pulled him out of his musings. "How are you coping with fixing meals?"

"Tonight, we're eating with Dad and Isabel," he said. "I want her to stay in close touch with them. But tomorrow night, I'll be cooking—under Dawn's supervision."

She smiled. "That's funny."

Yes, it was. "The problem is what to do after dinner. How do I entertain her?"

"You can explore your yard with the book," she suggested.

"Terrific idea." That should occupy an hour or two. "And we can write about it to Barbara."

"Also a chance for Dawn to practice her writing skills."

"Right." So they'd come up with enough activities to fill

one evening. That only left 364 in the year. "Any suggestions for what we can do on Wednesday?"

"Edmond!" Melissa started to lean forward, then cried out.

For a shocked moment, he feared she was suffering premature labor and might lose the babies. The intensity of his dread surprised him. So did the fact that he pictured the triplets for the first time not as blurry squiggles but as small precious girls like Dawn. Well, that's what they would be, eventually.

"Don't panic," she said, smiling. "Just normal aches and pains again."

"What a relief."

"I was about to point out that you don't have to entertain children every minute," Melissa said. "Dawn's seven, not a toddler. Once you share the book with her, let her poke around the yard on her own."

"Unsupervised?"

"The yard is fenced," Melissa said. "If you prefer, you can sit on the patio or watch from the kitchen."

"I suppose she is old enough for that. Still, I'll keep a close eye on her until I know her better." After all, Edmond had never anticipated Dawn would cook breakfast on her own. Who could guess what else she might do? "Now I have clients to meet and I'm sure you do, too."

"Pardon me if I don't stand up."

Rising, he came around the desk for a quick kiss. "I'll let you know if there's any news about my father's condition."

"Please do. I've been reluctant to trouble Isabel."

As soon as he left, he thought of a dozen other things to mention, the kind of small matters that married couples discussed over breakfast or supper. Would the two of them ever be like that again?

Edmond set the thought aside. Obviously, events had made that impossible.

MELISSA COULD HAVE sworn she had read fear on her ex-husband's face in response to her cramp. Had that been purely for her safety, or for the babies, too?

Being around Dawn was changing him or, she believed, bringing out a capacity for fatherhood he'd long suppressed. Edmond cared deeply about his sister, but taking on responsibility for her too young and then running head-on into her teen rebellion had apparently convinced him that parenting brought only disappointment and stress.

Damn his stubbornness! If only he wasn't too stubborn to see what was so obvious to her. Maybe then they could all be a family....

Voices in the outer office reminded Melissa that she had clients arriving, and her daydreams were getting her nowhere. Opening the notes in her computer, she prepared to guide another couple on their journey to parenthood.

Chapter Fifteen

"What kind of butterfly is that?" Peering into the bushes in the early-evening twilight, Dawn squinted through the camera. It had been her idea to take pictures for her letter to her mother.

Edmond searched fruitlessly for a matching shot in the book. "The plain white kind," he improvised. "Or else it's a moth."

"Uncle Eddie!" she protested as she pressed the button. "Try harder."

With a sigh, he flipped further into the book. They'd had fun cooking dinner. Dawn had showed him how to stir the pasta and how long to heat the sauce in the microwave. He'd demonstrated tossing the salad, and although some had landed on the floor, he'd been rewarded when she discovered that, to her surprise, she liked salad—with a generous dose of ranch dressing.

Afterward, Edmond had been intrigued by the first half hour of insect-watching, mostly because of Dawn's excitement. After a long day at the office, however, his energy was lagging.

"We might have to wait till tomorrow to find out what it is," he said. "We can ask Peter at sports camp."

"You promised we'd write Mommy tonight!"

Although Barbara wouldn't care whether they identified the butterfly, it mattered to Dawn, so he tried again.

Peering at the book in the fading light, Edmond spotted a prospect. "Here! It's a Cabbage White butterfly."

Dawn studied the page. "It's pretty."

"Yes, but it's a pest," Edmond noted, reading the text. "The larvae—the baby caterpillars—eat vegetables."

"So do we," his niece retorted. "Does that make us pests?"

He laughed. "You have an unusual view of the world." Still, it was getting late. "Now that we've identified it, let's go write the letter."

"Okay." Dawn might be stubborn, but she complied readily when he proposed something she'd enjoy.

Inside, they downloaded the picture to Edmond's laptop, where he opened a blank document. The completed letter would be printed out and sent by regular mail.

He wished phone calls were allowed, but Barbara was still awaiting assignment to a specific prison. Much as he wanted assurance of how she was doing, he was grateful she'd requested no visits until she was settled. The long drive would be grueling, especially while he and Dawn were establishing a routine.

He helped his niece insert the photo into the document and let her write about their insect hunt, taking over only when she became frustrated by her mistakes. Also, he told his sister that their father had set up an appointment with a specialist.

During dinner with his parents last night, only Dawn's chatter about sports camp had prevented an awkward silence. Mort had been withdrawn and ill-tempered, while Isabel had been unusually low-spirited. Edmond omitted that from the letter, though.

After they proofread, printed and signed it, Dawn kept flexing her fingers. "Is there something else you'd like to write?" Edmond asked as he folded the paper into an envelope.

"I wish I could write to Daddy." She shot him an apprehensive glance.

Edmond weighed how to respond. Much as he'd despised Simon, the man had been Dawn's father. Recalling that Dr. Brightman had urged him to validate whatever emotions she experienced, he said, "You must miss him."

"Yes." Sitting at the kitchen table where they'd been working, she stared down at her hands. "Is it wrong to love somebody who did bad things?"

"Feelings aren't right or wrong. They're natural, and they're okay." Therapy had taught him that. "You told me once that you were mad at your daddy. You aren't still angry?"

"I got mad when he was mean, but he could be nice, too." Tears trembled on her eyelashes as she gazed up at her uncle.

That raised a topic that worried Edmond, even though Dr. Brightman had detected no indications of abuse. "Did he ever hit you, or touch you in a way that was uncomfortable?"

She blinked, frowning. "He just yelled when I got in the way."

"Anything else?" He waited, in case she had more to say.

Out the rear window, he had a view of the darkening rear yard, with only a few lights from neighboring houses peeping through the bushes. What a peaceful place, the opposite of the apartment complex where he'd once visited Dawn and his sister. Graffiti had festooned the walls, angry voices had echoed, and a couple of slouching teenagers in gang-style clothing had lounged out front, watching Edmond as if weighing whether he posed a threat. Or perhaps whether they wanted to threaten him.

"Daddy took me to meet Santa Claus at the mall." Dawn's little chest heaved. "He said he always wished his daddy had done that for him."

Even that crook Simon had once been a vulnerable child, Edmond reflected. "If you want, I'll take you to the mall next Christmas."

She nodded. "I'd like that."

Abruptly, Edmond recalled a holiday when he'd escorted Barbara to the North Pole display at the mall while their mother was buying Christmas presents. Although his sister had been older than Dawn was now, her face had shone the same way, full of innocence and trust. *If she went so wrong despite my best efforts to guide her, how can I be sure Dawn's life won't get messed up, too?*

He'd put that question to Franca a few weeks ago, hoping for a definitive answer. The counselor's response had been that each person reacts differently to adolescence. Even the most ideal parents have no guarantee of how a child will develop.

Edmond closed his laptop. If only he could wrap Dawn in a cocoon and keep her safe until she was grown.

"Can Aunt Lissa come over?" she asked out of the blue. "I want to see how the babies are growing."

He searched for an excuse. "Honey, she shouldn't do any extra driving while she's pregnant."

"Then let's go over there."

He was tired of beating around the bush. And hadn't he resolved to be honest with her? "Remember at breakfast yesterday, when we talked about rules?" he said.

Dawn pressed her lips together. "Mmm-hmm."

"This isn't exactly a rule," Edmond admitted. "But Dr. Brightman believes it's important for you and me to spend time alone together, without anyone else. You've lost your dad and have to live apart from your mom. I'm the person who'll always be here for you."

"But can't I still see my aunt?" she asked earnestly.

"Yes, occasionally. But Dr. Brightman's afraid you'll be hurt when Aunt Lissa gets busy with the triplets."

"I can help," Dawn assured him. "In our old apartment, I used to babysit for the lady next door."

"You did?" Surely neither the mother nor Barbara had been negligent enough to leave this child alone with an infant. "By yourself?"

"I mean, while Mrs. Lawrence was napping," Dawn clarified. "She showed me how to change Ginny's diaper and feed her a bottle, too."

"Ah." He supposed that was all right, as long as the mother had been on the premises. "Mrs. Lawrence must have been fond of you."

"When she was pregnant, I rubbed her feet," Dawn continued proudly. "Can I do that for Aunt Lissa?"

"Let's not give Family Services the idea we're treating you as a servant." And now for a distraction. "How about some popcorn?"

"Sure."

Among Melissa's purchases had been an air popper and a jar of popping corn. "Let's fix a bowlful and eat it while we play with your jigsaw puzzle." A gift from her grandparents last night, it featured a colorful image of fish swimming through a coral reef. The printing inside the lid contained facts about tropical fish and coral.

Dawn scrunched her face. "Our hands will be greasy with butter. We'll mess up the puzzle."

"Good point. Let's work on it for a while and then break for popcorn."

"Okay."

They set it up on the coffee table, where they could leave the puzzle in place until it was finished. Edmond showed his niece the trick of finding the edge pieces first, and she concentrated intently.

Nearly an hour later, when they paused for a snack, Edmond realized he was enjoying himself. But eventually

Dawn would feel secure enough to challenge him, and he still had no idea how to respond.

DESPITE HER CURIOSITY about how Edmond and Dawn were faring on their second night alone, Melissa resisted the urge to call on Wednesday. If only she could magically peek in to make sure everything was going well.

She understood it was important for Edmond to relate to his niece without her running interference. But didn't she belong anywhere in the equation? Maybe he couldn't love the triplets but…but, then again, why couldn't he?

She supposed she ought to be reasonable. But she'd spent a lifetime being reasonable. It was wearing thin.

Melissa had just slipped into her nightgown when her phone sounded. His name on the readout gave her a buzz, just as it had when they were first dating.

Sitting at her desk chair, she asked, "How'd it go?"

"It's ridiculous to be pleased about such a small thing, but I was able to let her play in the yard while I fixed dinner." Amusement infused Edmond's voice. "I only checked on her every five minutes."

"Lucky you didn't burn the food."

"It's hard to burn beef stew," he said.

"No, it isn't." She'd done that once, shocked to discover that despite the liquid, the ingredients stuck to the bottom of the pot. "Dare I ask if you made it from scratch?"

"Yes," Edmond replied cheerily. "I believe that was the name on the label."

"What else did you do?" Every detail fascinated her.

"We made progress on the puzzle," he recounted. "Then we knocked off to read aloud."

"Something educational?"

"The newspaper," he replied.

"Seriously?" That might be rather deep for a seven-year-old. "Which section?"

Edmond cleared his throat. "The comics." The *Orange County Register* ran two pages of them daily, in color.

"Of course."

"I never figured fatherhood could be this fun," he said. "But Dr. Brightman cautioned that there'd be a honeymoon period, and I guess this is it. What if we clash in the long run?"

"You and she have a lot in common," Melissa ventured.

"Aside from our relatives, name three things."

"You're both smart." That was easy. "You have strong personalities."

"And?"

"And you both have the good taste to like me."

He chuckled. "Very much. Oops. She just got up to use the bathroom. If she suspects you're on the phone, she'll insist on talking to you, and then she'll never get to sleep."

Reluctantly, she acquiesced. "Sleep well."

"You, too." He clicked off.

From the next room, Melissa heard Karen and Rod laughing together. They weren't lovers yet, as far as she knew, but they grew closer almost daily.

How lovely to be at that stage of a relationship, when the future spread before you filled with possibilities. Those possibilities were still there for her and Edmond, if he would quit being so hardheaded.

But they were making progress. She hoped so, anyway. Or else she was setting herself up for another crushing disappointment.

DURING EDMOND'S SCHEDULED hospital hours on Thursday afternoon, Melissa was tempted to venture up to the fifth floor and poke her nose into his office, but her increasing size made every excursion a major effort. Stretching, she rubbed her sore abdomen.

At twenty weeks she was only halfway through a full-term pregnancy, yet she was already as large as many women at forty weeks. She'd be glad when she finally held these babies in her arms.

A tap drew her attention to Caroline's anxious face at the door. "Were you expecting Mr. Grant?"

Melissa hadn't been in touch with her daughters' genetic parents for weeks. "No. Is Nell here, too?"

"Just him," Caroline said. "And he seems agitated."

"About what?"

Rolling her eyes to signal that she didn't dare say more, the receptionist stepped aside. The man who stalked past her gave the impression he'd have thrust the other woman out of his path had she not moved.

Melissa avoided reacting to his body language. "Vern. Welcome!"

He glared at Caroline. "Privacy, please."

The young woman's gaze met Melissa's, silently asking permission. Receiving a nod, she scooted out and closed the door.

"What's up?" Although his attitude alarmed her, Melissa kept her tone pleasant.

"We want our babies back."

"What?"

Vern scowled. "You took advantage of us."

Dread squeezed her throat at the accusation. This had to be a misunderstanding. Or a bad dream. "Why would you say that?"

"My wife's in tears every night." He paced across the office, his light brown hair disheveled—a contrast to his usually trim appearance.

"What's wrong?" Melissa noted dark circles under the man's eyes. Caring for seven-month-old triplets must be stressful, yet sleep deprivation alone couldn't account for his barging in and throwing around wild claims.

"What's wrong?" he repeated mockingly. "You took our girls, that's what's wrong."

"I took your girls?" She felt foolish, echoing his words, but the charge blindsided her.

"You caught us in a weak moment." He planted himself in front of her with his hands in fists. "You were desperate for babies and you manipulated us into giving you ours."

His unfairness was so shocking that she hardly knew where to start. "I was far from desperate. As far as I'm aware, I could have conceived on my own."

He leaped to another point of attack. "You saw how cute our babies were, and you wanted our embryos for yourself."

"Vern, please sit down." Arguing was fruitless. They needed to get to the root of this situation. "Where's Nell? She should be part of this discussion."

"There's nothing to discuss," he snarled, still on his feet. "When our daughters are born, you're handing them over to us."

Aghast, Melissa gripped the edge of the desk. "These are my daughters now. You signed a contract."

"Under duress."

She blinked in astonishment. "What duress?"

Vern resumed pacing. "What you did was wrong. You played us."

As much as Melissa tried to remain objective, she couldn't. "The embryo transfer was your suggestion, yours and Nell's, not mine."

"That isn't true." A muscle bulged in his jaw. "My wife and I would never have agreed to give away our daughters if we'd been thinking straight. You were supposed to be there for us, not for your own gain."

Did he speak even a grain of truth? Melissa tried to recall what they'd said at the time, but her brain refused to cooperate. One matter stood out, however. "You and Nell insisted I decide immediately or you threatened to choose someone else."

He ignored the remark. "I could go to the administrator and have you fired for unethical conduct, but I'll give you a chance to fix this. You have until tomorrow to tear up that contract and agree to our terms." With that, he pivoted and stomped out.

Melissa could hardly breathe. Of all the possible problems that might arise, it had never occurred to her that the Grants would try to claim her daughters and threaten her career.

Overwhelmed, she burst into tears.

"IT'S NOT AS unusual as you might imagine," Edmond told the clients seated across from him. "About a quarter of surrogates are friends or relatives."

Bev and Mick Landry, the couple he'd met a few weeks earlier while they were conferring with Melissa, had scheduled the meeting to ask about Bev's younger sister serving as their surrogate.

"I'd feel more comfortable sharing the pregnancy with my sister than with a stranger," Bev said.

"Let's review the issues." Edmond brought up the question of whether Bev's sister would use her own eggs and whether her insurance would pay part of the medical expenses. They'd also have to resolve in advance how they'd respond if anything went wrong with the baby, whether the brother-in-law fully agreed to the surrogacy, and what they'd tell the child about her "aunt."

"This sure is complicated," Mick grumbled.

"Of course it's complicated," his wife said. "Most people would think we're weird for even considering it."

"There's a surrogate mother in the Bible, so it's not that weird," her husband retorted.

"On the other hand, I don't recall anybody suing anybody in the Bible, which is why I advise covering all the bases," Edmond answered calmly. "It would be wise to draw up a contract, including what expenses you'll pay and whether your sister-in-law will have visitation rights. Both sides should bring their own lawyer, and your brother-in-law should sign the surrogacy agreement also."

Bev toyed with her purse strap. "Could we hire you as our attorney?"

"Certainly, but in my private practice. I'm only a consultant at the hospital." Quickly Edmond added, "Or I'd be happy to suggest other family law firms in the area." While part of his motive in affiliating with the hospital had been to expand his business, it was important that clients chose the representation that suited them best.

When the couple departed, it was almost five o'clock. He wouldn't mind picking up Dawn earlier than scheduled, especially since this was their evening to visit the therapist, but first he checked his email. There was welcome news: Portia Adams had agreed to his suggestion of a playdate for the girls.

"Saturday morning at the Oahu Lane Shelter is fine," she'd written. "However, a certain person volunteers there in the afternoon and we do not want to run into him."

That would be Rod, Edmond reflected. He typed a quick response, promising to set up the volunteer stint at a time when they wouldn't run into "a certain person."

He pressed Send and had begun collecting his belongings when his phone rang—Melissa.

Smiling, he answered, "Hi."

"Can you come down?" A sob shook her voice. "Something awful has happened."

"I'm on my way." Barely pausing to click off the phone, he sprinted for the stairs.

Chapter Sixteen

The urgency in Melissa's words flooded Edmond with fear. He had to force himself to slow for a gurney in the corridor, barely avoided skidding down the last flight of stairs, and raced through the empty reception area where Caroline usually sat.

His heart was still pounding when he entered Melissa's office. It was a relief to find her sitting upright rather than lying down, screaming in pain, as he'd feared. "Are you okay?"

"I didn't mean to scare you." Sniffing, she wiped her eyes on a tissue. Her skin was unusually pale, he noted. "Thanks for coming. Do you need to pick up Dawn?"

"Not yet." Keeping track of his niece's schedule was becoming instinctive. "What happened?"

Her voice breaking, she described a threatening visit from Vern Grant. The man was completely out of line, in Edmond's opinion.

"I don't think they can force me to do anything but I'm not sure," she concluded.

"Legally, you're the mother." Edmond had researched the subject after learning the facts of Melissa's pregnancy. "Embryos are considered property, and the Grants transferred ownership to you. They can't simply change their minds, walk in here and demand the babies."

"Vern just did." She hurried on. "Whatever the law says,

he contends I took advantage of him and Nell when they were vulnerable. Given my position of trust here at the hospital, I'm terrified he might have a case."

"Didn't you say the embryo transfer was their idea?" It infuriated Edmond that the man had hurled such accusations and upset Melissa in her condition. Or any condition.

"Yes, but…" She released a ragged breath. "Even if they can't win in court, they could wreck my reputation. I hope Mark would stand by me, but he has to answer to a corporation based on the other side of the country. And if this damages the hospital's reputation, I'd feel awful."

Now that he'd learned she was in no immediate danger, Edmond's wrath focused on the person who'd put her in this position. "What he's saying could be considered slander."

"So I should spend years and all my money suing him?" Melissa asked. "Even if I won, between the internet and the press, it'd still ruin my career."

His outrage refused to yield. "One might make a case that they manipulated *you* into serving as their surrogate, without your consent."

"I don't believe they planned this," she said unhappily. "But there's no time for tempers to cool. They're insisting that I agree to their terms by tomorrow."

"What terms?" Edmond countered.

"Tear up the contract and give them my babies." The devastation on her face cut him to the core.

"What about your terms?" he responded. "Even if you went along, which you won't, are they proposing to pay for your lost work and suffering? Surrogates are paid between twenty and forty thousand dollars, plus expenses."

He paused, aware that he was letting his emotions control him. Melissa had a right to his best advice and clearest thinking.

"I hadn't considered that." She folded her arms as if holding in her emotions. "I want to fight, only I keep see-

ing their side of this, too. They must miss their little girls,
now that their little boys are getting bigger."

Edmond ached to defend her with all his expertise, but
this wasn't his decision. Also, he still believed in collaborative rather than adversarial family law, even with people
who ticked him off.

Reaching across the desk, he stroked her hands. "As
soon as fire stops shooting out of my ears, I'll call the
Grants and suggest we meet. I'll explain that I'm attending as your friend, but that they're welcome to bring an attorney if they'd like."

"My schedule's packed tomorrow," Melissa said worriedly. "But if necessary, I'll rearrange it."

"This weekend should be soon enough. As you said,
everyone's tempers need to cool." He'd find a sitter for his
niece. That raised another point. "We should avoid mentioning this to Dawn. This is a touchy subject."

"Especially while it's unresolved." Tears flowed down
her cheeks again. "It feels like a judgment. I've wondered
if I'm capable of caring for three babies."

"If you weren't frightened about raising triplets by yourself, you wouldn't be human," Edmond assured her. "But
you aren't by yourself anymore. I'll support whatever you
choose."

Melissa's mouth quirked with a hint of a smile. "I appreciate that."

A few minutes later, possessed of the Grants' phone
number and with Melissa in slightly better spirits, Edmond
headed for his office. As he climbed the stairs to burn off
nervous energy, he recalled his impulsive statement that
he'd support whatever she chose. Melissa must be wondering what he meant by that, and in truth, so was he.

He'd begun to imagine a future in which he and Dawn
frequently visited Melissa and her babies. He'd pictured

the triplets becoming toddlers, old enough to read stories to and play games with.

But that didn't mean he could be their father. Despite his progress with Dawn, Edmond wasn't convinced he could succeed with even one child. But it was unthinkable for Melissa to be forced to give up the daughters she loved.

At his office, he decided he'd calmed enough to place the call. Besides, the Grants had set tomorrow as a deadline, which meant he'd better contact them before then.

Holding himself steady, Edmond dialed their number.

THAT NIGHT, MELISSA barely touched her dinner. Luckily, Jack and Anya had joined the group and the conversation flowed merrily around her. The newlyweds laughed a lot and occasionally finished each other's sentences as they recounted their adventures snorkeling and swimming on Catalina Island.

Only a little over a month from her due date, Anya also reported on the flood of gifts from her large family for baby Rachel Lenore. "There's more clothing than she can possibly wear," she told Zora and Melissa. "I'll share them with you guys, although you'll probably be inundated, as well."

"I'll organize a shower in September." Karen slanted a concerned glance at Melissa. She'd been the only one at the table who'd noticed her friend's withdrawal that evening.

"What a great idea." Anya bubbled over with ideas. Even Zora, whose pregnancy weighed more and more on her mind as well as on her body, brightened at the prospect of games, refreshments and a party at the house.

Melissa held it together until the newlyweds, Lucky and Zora went out to a movie. Then she collapsed on the couch in the den, ready to explode into a thousand pieces.

Karen joined her. "You're upset. I presume this has to do with Vern Grant's visit this afternoon."

Melissa stretched along the couch to elevate her feet. "Caroline told you?"

"She was worried." Sheepishly, her friend admitted, "And I heard raised voices. Not the words, but the general tone." While the walls between offices were thick enough for privacy, they weren't soundproof.

"Caroline means well, but please don't repeat any of this to her." It would be awful if her plight became gossip.

"Of course not." Glancing toward the kitchen, where Rod's dishwashing activities had grown suspiciously quiet, Karen called, "House rules forbid repeating anything you overhear, Rod."

His inquisitive face poked through the doorway. "Since you bring it up, I might as well join you." Removing his apron, he added, "I'm done in the kitchen."

Melissa wasn't thrilled about sharing confidences with a third party. However, since Rod had been deprived of his daughters, he might have insight into her situation.

She repeated Vern's claims and Edmond's comments. "Edmond emailed to say they've agreed to meet us tomorrow night at their house. They didn't say if they're bringing a lawyer."

"On a Friday evening?" Rod quirked an eyebrow. "It'd be a wonder if they found one of those bottom feeders to work such odd hours."

"Rod!" Karen narrowed her eyes at him.

"I didn't mean Edmond," he amended.

"Besides, the Grants don't have a lot of money." *Which might give them an additional motive to sue me,* Melissa reflected unhappily.

"I'll watch Dawn," Karen offered.

"Thanks. I'll let Edmond know." She sorted through her turbulent thoughts. "I keep wondering... *Did* I do something wrong? It's true that they suggested the embryo transfer, but I could have refused."

"As I recall, they pressured you," Karen said loyally.

"All the same, I was in a position of trust." Inside Melissa, flutterings indicated the girls were playing again. She hugged herself, hoping the little ones sensed the strength of her love.

"The embryo transfer happened after their sons were born, right?" Rod didn't wait for confirmation. "Seems to me you'd fulfilled your responsibilities as a counselor."

"Except that the embryos were at Safe Harbor, which means the Grants were still our clients." Her chest felt heavy. "If I'd been more objective, maybe I'd have stepped aside."

"But they'd already ruled out bearing the children themselves, hadn't they?" Karen probed.

"That's true."

"Had they chosen to donate to anyone else, they'd have never dared make a claim like this," Karen said.

Melissa wished the matter were that simple. "Maybe not, but I put myself in this situation by acting on impulse."

"These people changed their minds, pure and simple," Rod chimed in. "If you ask me, they're taking advantage of *your* vulnerability. They assume they can manipulate you into giving them what they couldn't afford and weren't willing to risk themselves."

His dismissive tone, Melissa suspected, sprang from resentment at his ex-wife's betrayal and the loss of Tiffany and Amber. He'd only reconnected with them this year after Tiffany ran away from San Diego to see him and her grandmother, who lived in Safe Harbor. Since the grandmother had a fondness for her former son-in-law, she occasionally arranged for Rod to join her and the girls, without the parents' knowledge, although Portia must suspect.

She *had* persuaded her husband that there was no harm in allowing Tiffany and Amber to be flower girls at Jack's wedding, since he'd been close when they were little. But in Melissa's opinion, Portia and Vince simply liked to act important at social events, especially those involving the hospital staff.

What if her own daughters grew up amid court battles and conflicting claims? The legal fight had drained Rod's savings. If Melissa lost hers, how would she raise three children?

"Surely the Grants will come around." Karen's guarded optimism contrasted with Rod's skepticism.

Melissa shivered. "I'm dreading tomorrow night."

"You'll do fine," Karen said. "Edmond will be with you."

"Yes." That was the one positive note in this experience.

Rod's phone beeped with a text. "It's Tiff," he reported. "The girls are spending the night at their Grandma Helen's house and the coast is clear."

"Helen invited us over for game night," Karen explained. "I hate sneaking around to see the girls, but the Adamses leave us no choice."

"I don't hate sneaking around," Rod responded cheerfully. "I enjoy it."

"Because you're thumbing your nose at Vince," Karen said wryly.

"You bet."

To Melissa, Karen asked, "Are you okay alone? I don't have to go."

"I'm fine." To forestall further offers, she said, "Go! I insist."

The house fell quiet after they departed. Gazing through the glass doors into the summer night, Melissa had a startling idea.

Fate had presented her with a strange opportunity, if she chose to view it that way. Saying yes to the Grants might not only save her career, it might also clear a path for her and Edmond to be a couple again. To be a family with Dawn.

A wave of despair washed over her. *I can't give them up. They're my daughters.*

Melissa had always been sensible, and tonight the arguments lined up like bowling pins. But her heart ordered her to throw the ball and smash them to bits.

To hell with being sensible.

THRILLED TO SEE her aunt on Friday even though she'd been warned that Melissa and Edmond had to leave after dinner, Dawn bounced in her chair through the meal at Karen's house.

"What do the triplets look like?" she asked eagerly.

"They're about six inches long," her aunt said. "And— Oh, you mean what *will* they look like when they're older?"

"Yes!"

If this was a touchy subject for her, Melissa hid it well, Edmond reflected. "They'll probably be blonde, but they aren't identical. That means they were born from separate eggs, so they'll be as different as any three sisters. One might have darker hair, for instance."

"I'll bet they'll be cute," Dawn said.

"No cuter than you."

The little girl beamed.

Edmond saw no harm in bringing his niece to visit her aunt after keeping them apart all week. Dawn was doing well in her new home, as Dr. Brightman had agreed at Thursday's consultation.

"We aren't out of the woods yet," she'd told Edmond. "But you're handling this very well." Strangely, the praise mattered more to him than the fact that his law practice was growing and that he'd received compliments from both Geoff and Tony this week.

Tonight, however, Edmond was entering alien territory. If only he had some idea what to expect at the meeting with the Grants. On the phone, Vern had been calmer than Melissa described him, but there was little chance he'd changed his mind. He might even have hired an attack-dog attorney to lie in wait for them.

Should that happen, Edmond would have to work at controlling his temper. The saying went, "An attorney who represents himself has a fool for a client." But he was only participating as Melissa's friend. If this matter did end up in court, he'd hire someone who didn't have a personal stake in the outcome.

After dinner, Edmond reminded Dawn that he and Aunt Lissa had adult business to take care of.

"Karen borrowed some games from Tiffany and Amber," she said. "We'll have fun."

"I'm sure you will." He hugged her.

"Thanks for babysitting," Melissa told her friends. "I owe you."

"No, you don't," Karen answered. "We'll enjoy this."

Assisting Melissa along the driveway to his car, Edmond noticed how much larger she'd become—again. "Are you sure you're well enough for this?"

Melissa adjusted a clip in her hair. "Yes. I'm still able to work, remember? Although I'll start riding with Karen on Monday."

"I approve." He'd have offered to drive her himself, but he had to take Dawn to sports camp. And starting in a few weeks, to school.

In the car, Edmond navigated across town toward the address Vern Grant had provided. "I wish you'd reconsider about formulating a strategy," he said. Melissa had declined his earlier suggestion to discuss tactics.

"I'd rather just listen to them." In the fading light— the days seemed shorter already, although July had barely yielded to August—her gaze sought his for understanding.

"You're more comfortable relying on intuition," Edmond

summarized. "It's still best to have an opening gambit, a fallback position and a bottom line."

"How do you strategize options about losing the children you love?" She rested her forehead against the passenger window. "The opening gambit, the fallback position and the bottom line are all the same. My answer is no."

"We used to discuss best and worst case scenarios in difficult situations, remember?" *Until the divorce, anyway.* "That helped prepare us."

"Sure, like when we heard my parents were in an accident in Hawaii," Melissa said bleakly. "Best case scenario was that they'd recover. But we got our worst case." Her mother had died a few hours after arriving at the hospital, while her father had passed the next morning.

"But it gave us a chance to research how to handle funeral arrangements while we were still in a hopeful mood," he pointed out.

She sighed. "This isn't making me feel any better, Eddie."

"I guess not." Weaving through the Friday evening traffic on Safe Harbor Boulevard, he searched for a way to lighten her mood. "If something goes wrong, it doesn't have to be the end of your dream of becoming a mother."

"Doesn't it?" she asked tearfully. "If I lost my little girls, I'm not sure I could go through another pregnancy."

That heartbroken expression on her face tore at Edmond. These children meant the world to her. She was their mother. But he was not their father, and he reminded himself that the best way to help Melissa and the triplets was to remain impartial, even if he wanted to defend them to the ends of the earth.

He halted the car in front of a one-story bungalow with shutters and a wide porch. Such a pretty place. But they were facing a scene that might not be pretty at all.

Determined, he got out and circled to help Melissa.

Chapter Seventeen

Vern didn't immediately launch into an attack as he admitted them, but his taut body language told Melissa he hadn't lost his determination. Holding on to Edmond's arm, she gazed around their small living room, which she'd never visited before.

Playpens, stuffed animals, a changing station and a bounce chair obscured whatever the décor had been pre-parenthood, while the scents of baby powder and laundry soap lingered in the air. Nell sat on the carpet watching a blond baby creep toward a glittery ball.

The new mom rose, revealing a tall, slightly pudgy figure, and removed a towel from her shoulder. "The other two went to sleep, but Tommy's our explorer." Nell brushed back short hair a shade lighter than Melissa's. She'd cut her once-flowing locks during her pregnancy.

"They never all sleep at once," Vern said. "It must violate their union rules."

Edmond gave a polite chuckle. Melissa wasn't sure how to respond. In the past, she'd joked and chatted with the Grants like a close friend. Now, she hesitated about what to say. Who could tell what remark might set off a tirade of accusations?

"May I sit down?" she asked.

"Of course." Nell hurried to remove a baby blanket from

the couch. "My gosh, you're huge. How far along are you? I've forgotten."

"Almost five months." Melissa lowered herself to the seat. "I have to stop driving soon. You remember that stage."

"I'd put it out of my mind." Nell glanced uncertainly at Edmond. "You're her ex-husband?"

"I'm here as a friend." He stood with hands clasped in front of him. But behind those glasses, his brain was measuring and assessing. While Melissa appreciated his analytical powers, she'd much rather be assured that he was fiercely in her court, committed to her and to the babies. "Is anyone else joining us?" An attorney, he meant.

"It's just us," Nell said.

"We can speak for ourselves," her husband added with a touch of belligerence.

On the floor, Tommy scooted for the ball. It rolled a few inches off, arousing a dismayed grunt from the child. Another scoot, and the ball rolled again. The baby's complaint rose to a wail.

Vern scooped him up. "Can't have him waking the others," he said. Nell stretched her shoulders and neck.

Melissa decided to raise the painful subject that had brought them here. "I was surprised to hear from Vern yesterday," she ventured.

"I didn't know he intended to drop in on you," Nell said.

Melissa doubted Vern had acted without some encouragement from his wife. "He indicated you've been upset."

"That's right." Vern adjusted the baby on his shoulder. "She misses her little girls."

Edmond's eyes narrowed. He was probably wondering how the woman could miss what she'd never had. But before this pregnancy, Melissa had missed having a child, so she understood.

Don't be too understanding. You're not here as their advocate.

"It's been hard caring for triplets, I won't pretend otherwise." Nell perched on the arm of the couch. "But that doesn't mean I've forgotten my other babies."

These are no longer your babies, she thought, struggling against a flare of temper, but Nell's attention was fixed on Melissa's belly. "How are the girls doing?"

"Fine."

"Can I feel them?"

Edmond took a step forward as if to block any such attempt. Much as Melissa appreciated his protectiveness, she doubted it could do any harm. "Go ahead."

Easing down beside her, Nell laid her palm on Melissa's bulge. After waiting a minute, the other woman appeared disappointed. "Nothing going on right now, huh?"

"Sorry, they're not being very active at the moment."

Nell removed her hand. "They'll soon be active all the time. I want to be part of this."

"Excuse me?" Melissa asked.

Nell took a deep breath. "Giving away our daughters— I wasn't thinking clearly. And to a single mom! The girls deserve a father."

"I raised that point myself." Melissa couldn't believe the woman was revisiting the issue now. "You said it didn't matter."

Nell cleared her throat. "You should have counseled us to keep our options open, that we might change our minds."

Melissa strained to hold in her frustration. "I did."

Vern glared. "Like hell!"

Edmond raised a cautionary hand. "Let's keep this civil, shall we?"

The two men faced each other as if they were a pair of, well, male animals. Edmond had never been hotheaded, however, and luckily Tommy's fussing distracted Vern.

"I reviewed my notes today," Melissa said, glad she'd kept careful records. "I advised you repeatedly that frozen embryos can remain viable for years. However, you informed me if I didn't take them during my next cycle, you'd find another recipient."

"It hurt to picture them cold and alone," Nell admitted, then put in, "I might have been suffering from postpartum blues, which you should have understood."

"I asked you about signs of depression. You denied experiencing any. All the same, I urged you to consult a counselor before deciding what to do with the embryos."

"I don't remember any of that," Vern said.

"Neither do I." Nell lifted her chin. "Those are our daughters you're carrying, our genetic children. From now on, Vern or I will attend all your doctor's appointments and ensure you're eating the right diet. When the girls are born, we're taking them home. Otherwise we'll go to the hospital administrator and have you fired."

Intrude into her medical exams? Run her life and commandeer her children? Fury powered Melissa to her feet.

"What do you think I am, your slave?" she demanded. "Was this your scheme, to trick me into serving as your unpaid surrogate?"

She could see Edmond staring at her in surprise. And with a hint of admiration, too.

Nell's eyes widened in shock. "How can you accuse us of tricking you?"

"I never considered embryo adoption until you brought it up," Melissa retorted. "Then you pressured me to implant the embryos immediately."

"It was still your decision," Nell protested.

"You urged me to hold your little boys, when you should have realized that would remind me of how much I wanted a baby." Melissa had no idea where these words sprang from, but they kept flowing. "You told me you'd dreamed that I was meant to be the mother of these babies." She was so angry, her hands shook.

Edmond hurried to her side. "Your blood pressure might rise—"

"You bet it's rising!" Melissa roared. "These people are treating me like a brood mare and trying to steal my babies!"

Nell and Vern were speechless. Tommy had stopped squirming in his daddy's arms to gape at her.

"Let's table this discussion until we've all calmed down." Gently, Edmond drew her toward the door. "Mr. and Mrs. Grant, I'll call you tomorrow."

They nodded without a word.

Outside, the evening air cooled Melissa's skin. As they walked to the car, every twinge from her stretched abdomen reminded her of what she was enduring and risking for the sake of her daughters. How dare the Grants presume to attend her doctor visits and supervise her diet!

"I've never seen you like this," Edmond said as he held the car door for her.

"Neither have I." Once he was behind the wheel, she added, "I was fighting for my children."

He gave her a wry smile. "I'm impressed."

"Did I make things worse?" She recalled the outrage on the Grants' faces when she'd accused them of manipulation.

"Doubtful," Edmond said. "You stuck to the point and didn't throw in random accusations."

"The way Vern did in my office?" As they drove to her house, she reflected how sad it was that the Grants' contentions had destroyed her old sense of comfort around them. "What happens next?"

"Let's see how they react when I call," Edmond said. "Maybe they'll change their minds after hearing your side of the story."

Melissa shuddered. "They'll probably hire a lawyer, and

the next thing we hear he'll be in Mark Rayburn's office demanding my dismissal." Much as she hated dwelling on the negative, she had to prepare for that possibility.

"In my opinion, that would be a serious miscalculation on their part." He kept his attention on the spottily illuminated road. "They'd have more leverage by merely threatening to hire an attorney. Once they do, the hospital will be reluctant to admit any wrongdoing."

"Oh, that makes me a whole lot happier," she muttered.

"Sorry." With the car halted at a red light, Edmond turned his gaze on her. "Honey, the law's on your side. You're the girls' mother. I haven't reviewed the contract you and the Grants signed, but I'm assuming Tony drew it up, and he's damn smart."

She waited, hoping for more—a declaration that they'd get through this together, that he'd begun to feel something for the babies. *Tell me you've started to care about them.*

When he didn't, Melissa asked, "What if the law isn't enough? The Grants might not be able to take the babies, but they can ruin my career."

Edmond shrugged. "Worst case scenario, you might have to decide whether you'd rather lose the career you've worked for so hard, or relinquish the babies."

How could he placidly propose the devastation of her dreams? "I guess I should have expected that from you," Melissa snapped.

"I beg your pardon?" His mouth tightened.

"I must have been out of my mind, to imagine you and I could ever truly be close again." Anguish combined with her fury at the Grants, and she unleashed it all on this man for whom she'd risked her heart. "You still resent my request that we consider having children."

"Okay, I resented it," Edmond replied. "That doesn't mean I'm trying to punish you. One of us has to view things logically."

"That's right, I'm completely irrational." If he'd deliberately set out to infuriate her, he couldn't have done a better job. "The worst part is that you're lying to yourself. Anyone watching you with Dawn can tell you were meant to be a father."

"Now I'm the one who's irrational?" he asked grimly. "Despite everything I've experienced in my life, everything I've learned about myself, I'm clueless. Only you can show me the truth."

"That's about the size of it." Melissa clamped down on her impulse to shoot more barbs at him. Until tonight, she'd never imagined that she could speak to Edmond, or anyone, this way.

Now she'd destroyed whatever might have existed between them. But hadn't it only been a mirage, anyway?

Edmond remained silent, too, until they reached her driveway. "I'll call the Grants tomorrow."

"Thank you." She made her way into the house, declining his offer of help.

THAT NIGHT, AFTER Edmond read a story to Dawn and tucked her into bed, Melissa's tirade still twisted and burned inside him. She was more than a lover and more than a friend, she was the only person he'd ever truly opened up to and depended on. Now she'd rejected the person he knew himself to be.

He didn't deserve the anger she'd hurled at him, but he supposed she'd been holding some of that inside since he first informed her about the vasectomy. Had she lashed out then, would it have made any difference?

Instead, she'd sat frozen in shock. He'd probed for a reaction and tried to reassure her that he loved her. When she didn't respond, he'd hoped his words would gradually sink in.

The next day, he'd arrived home from work to find that

she'd moved out. From then on, she'd coolly handled the details of their divorce, avoiding any discussion of what had set it off. After a few attempts to persuade her into counseling, he'd accepted that their differences were irreconcilable.

In all honesty, even if she'd roared at him, Edmond doubted he'd have reversed the vasectomy. Despite his willingness to serve as Dawn's guardian and his desire to help Melissa through her pregnancy, he wasn't cut out for fatherhood. In bed, he tossed and turned until he finally fell into a troubled sleep.

On Saturday morning, Dawn grew overexcited with eagerness to join her new friends, asking every five minutes if they could leave yet. At nine o'clock, when they arrived at the Oahu Lane Shelter in a light industrial complex near the freeway, Edmond had to catch her arm to prevent her from dashing across the parking lot.

"Always look both ways," he warned. "Drivers can't see you."

"There they are!" Waving, she tugged against his grasp. "Tiffany! Amber!"

Beaming, the red-haired girls waved back. Their mother, a slender woman with auburn hair, nodded a greeting to Edmond, who had been introduced to her at the wedding. In her late thirties, Portia Adams wore a hot-pink designer jogging suit. Faded jeans might be more appropriate for today's outing, but Vince Adams's wife could afford to discard an expensive outfit if it got stained.

When they reached the rambling one-story building, a young woman in a blue blazer checked their names off a list. "Ilsa will be right with you," she said.

"Ilsa?" Portia asked.

"That's the shelter's director, Ilsa Ivy." Edmond had noticed the name on the website.

"She provides the orientation for new volunteers," the

blazer-clad woman said. "How many shifts a week do you plan to sign up for?"

It hadn't occurred to Edmond that they'd be expected to volunteer on a regular basis. "We're exploring our options."

"Can we come every Saturday, please, please?" Dawn peered into the hallway as if expecting little animals to trot into view. Judging by the chorus of yips and meows from within, there were quite a few on hand.

"I'll consider it," he told her. A regular volunteer shift might bring them closer, and the cause was worthwhile. However, once Barbara received her prison assignment, they'd have to take some Saturdays to visit her.

"I wish *we* could. But with school starting, we have to go back to San Diego." Amber made a face.

"We'll visit our grandma, though." Tiffany took Dawn's hand. "Like we did last night."

Portia gritted her teeth just as the shelter's director, a tall woman with thick gray hair, arrived to escort them and a handful of fellow newcomers through the building. She pointed out recent improvements.

"We now perform spay and neuter operations here on the premises, instead of transporting the animals to another location," she announced. "We're very grateful to have received a large donation."

Beside Edmond, Portia murmured, "I suppose we'll have to contribute something to keep the girls happy."

Politely, he said, "That's generous of you."

For the girls' sake and because she and her husband were important to Safe Harbor Medical, Edmond wished he could like this woman. That hope faded as the morning passed, however. She wrinkled her nose at the odors from the cages, although Edmond considered the shelter well maintained, and yawned openly while Ilsa explained the need for volunteers to foster animals.

"I wish we could adopt a kitten," Amber said wistfully

as they viewed a newly rescued litter. "We have room, Mommy."

"Please don't mention that idea to your father," Portia warned, nostrils flaring. "He hates cats."

"I heard you have a new house," Tiffany commented to Edmond. "You could get a pet."

"We're renting so we'd need the landlord's approval." He glanced at Dawn. Eventually, adopting an animal might be feasible, but not yet.

To his relief, she shook her head firmly. "We can't. I'll be too busy helping my aunt with the babies."

"You will?" Tiffany exchanged a look with her sister. Now, what was that about?

Ilsa paused at the end of the corridor. "We don't normally put volunteers to work without training, but we just received a large load of newspapers that have to be folded to fit inside cages."

Portia's expression grew pinched. "Does she seriously expect us to sit around folding newspapers all morning?"

"I'll talk to her." Portia's attitude irked him, but he *had* been the one to suggest they meet here.

As their group dispersed, Edmond took the director aside to apologize for bringing a guest who didn't understand what they'd be asked to do. When he mentioned that his companion was Mrs. Vince Adams, Ilsa gave a start of recognition.

"Actually, we could use her advice," she said, "We're planning a charity ball next Christmas and I'm sure she'd have great ideas."

Edmond thanked her. "I'm happy to fold newspapers."

"We'd appreciate it." The older woman smiled in approval. "As for the girls, they can play with some kittens who're ready for adoption."

Portia showed a spark of interest at Ilsa's request, especially when she learned that social leaders from Irvine and Newport Beach were expected to attend. By the time a teenage volunteer returned the girls an hour later with cat fur on their clothes, Portia had provided contact information and permission to use her and Vince's names as supporters of the shelter.

"Naturally, we'll send a donation," she informed Ilsa.

"That would be most appreciated."

As for Edmond, he didn't mind a few paper cuts and ink-smudged hands. After washing up, he shepherded the group out.

The girls hugged each other goodbye in the parking lot. Tiff and Amber were kind little souls, very different from their parents. Edmond credited their grandmother and Rod's influence during their early years.

Not being related genetically to his daughters obviously didn't matter to Rod. And the way Melissa had fought for her children last night showed as tight a bond as any mother had with an infant. He realized now that implying she might give them up had been ill advised, but he'd been thinking in terms of best and worst case scenarios.

Meeting the Grants—despite the unpleasant circumstances—along with their little boy had provided Edmond with a sharper picture of the tiny girls within Melissa. A scene flashed into his mind: his house filled with playpens and toys and three adorable girls rolling and crawling and clamoring for attention. How exhausting. But strangely appealing, too.

He gave a start. Had Melissa sensed that would be his reaction even before he did? Edmond respected her intuition in most instances. But then his mind conjured another image, of his sister, alone and scared in a prison cell. And his idle fantasy about babies fell apart in the face of his complete lack of understanding of where he'd gone wrong with Barbara.

He and Dawn were almost home before he noticed how

quiet she'd grown. "Did you have fun with your friends? It's obvious they care about you."

Staring out the window, Dawn shrugged.

Something had upset her, and he had no idea what. Grasping for straws, he asked, "Are you worried about the kittens finding homes? This is a no-kill shelter. They'll all be placed eventually."

Another shrug.

At their driveway, Edmond pressed the garage opener. "Honey, I can't read your mind. Can you say what's wrong?"

"Nothing." Her tearful tone belied the response.

"Obviously, something is." In his pocket, his phone sounded. What rotten timing! He couldn't ignore it, though, in case it was the Grants. Glancing at the readout once they were inside the garage, he saw his stepmother's name and grew concerned. Normally she only emailed about routine matters. "Isabel? What's up?"

Dawn opened the passenger door. Holding the phone, Edmond exited, too.

"Your father met with the specialist yesterday," Isabel said.

Damn! Events had pushed Mort's appointment from his mind. "What did you find out?" he asked as he let his niece into the house.

"There's good news, mostly."

"What do you mean, mostly?"

"Mort doesn't have dementia," Isabel said evenly.

"That's fantastic." A weight lifted from Edmond. Despite his preoccupation with more immediate issues, the prospect of his father's long-term decline had troubled him deeply. "Dad's okay, then?"

"Medically speaking, yes."

"What do you mean?" Peripherally, Edmond noticed

Dawn disappearing toward her bedroom, head down. Well, one crisis at a time.

There was a noise on the other hand, and his father's gruff voice spoke into his ear. "I'd better explain this myself, son."

Chapter Eighteen

Perplexed, Edmond paced through the front room. "What's this about, Dad?"

"Something I should have admitted years ago." His father sucked in a raspy breath. "I've let you carry too much of my burden."

Was he feeling guilty because he'd been away so much driving a truck? "You had to earn a living." Edmond pictured Mort's strong face with the etched lines of a smoker.

"I don't mean that," his father growled. "My diagnosis isn't dementia, it's something called pseudodementia. That means I act like I'm nuts, but I'm not."

"You don't act nuts." Realizing he should simply listen, Edmond said, "Go on."

"The specialist they sent me to was a shrink." His father pronounced the last word with disdain. Although he'd accepted Dawn's therapy, it wasn't the sort of thing Mort would have undergone himself. *Until now.* "He says I'm suffering from depression."

That was understandable. "It's been a rough year."

"Not the normal down-in-the-dumps kind," Mort said bitterly. "The kind that's been eating at me for years. The kind I deserve."

"You need to get something off your chest?"

"That's right. This was hard enough for me to tell the shrink and I'm only saying it to you once. So listen hard."

"I'm listening." Edmond wandered into the kitchen.

Gruffly, Mort described his sense of losing control with Barbara, then sixteen, after Edmond married and moved out. Although he'd switched jobs to be closer to home, Barb had acted like a stranger, plus he'd been dealing with his wife's cancer.

"Made me damn furious when your sister ran around, drinking and cutting school," he said. "I figured she was old enough to be a decent human being while her mother was sick." Their arguments had escalated, with commands and reproaches on Mort's side and defiance on Barbara's.

One afternoon after taking his wife to chemotherapy, Mort had driven home to pick up a book she'd forgotten and interrupted Barbara nearly naked on the front couch with her new boyfriend. The sight of Simon—covered with tattoos and obviously much older than her—had been the last straw.

Furious, he'd sent Simon away with threats to call the police. Then Mort had forbidden Barbara to see him again and grounded her for a month. She'd responded with a rude gesture and told him with a four-letter-word what he could do to himself.

"I lost it." Mort's voice tightened. "Took off my belt and lit into her."

"You didn't." Horrified, Edmond had an image of his outraged, hulking father beating his half-dressed sister.

"I stopped when I realized I'd raised welts on her back," his father said shakily. "She grabbed her clothes and ran to her room." Mort was breathing hard now. "I had to return to your mom at the infusion center. By the time we got home, Barbara had packed a suitcase and gone."

"That's why she left." Edmond had believed he was to blame for being selfishly wrapped up in his happy marriage. But why hadn't his sister confided in him? He'd tried to call her after she left, only to receive the cold-shoulder treatment.

"Simon took pictures of her welts and she threatened to report me to the police if I interfered again," Mort said angrily.

"No wonder you refused to act against Simon." On further reflection, Edmond supposed Barbara might have feared that if he learned the truth, he would report both Mort *and* Simon's misdeeds to the police. *Well, I might have. And if I had, maybe she wouldn't be in prison now.*

"She never felt she could return home, no matter how bad things got," Mort said unhappily. "Rotten as Simon was, I don't believe he ever beat her."

Edmond recalled Dawn saying her father had yelled at them, but nothing more. "I don't think so, either."

"That's the whole ugly story," Mort finished. "I've been holding it inside, and this past year, when everything blew up, it was driving me crazy. I couldn't focus on anything except how I drove your sister to this."

Dismayed as he was, Edmond couldn't let his father take all the blame. "Dad, Barbara's twenty-four years old and a mother. She should have had better sense than to take part in a robbery."

"I owe her a big apology," Mort said. "But there's no undoing the damage."

"An apology would be a start." Aware of how difficult this conversation had been, Edmond said, "Thanks for telling me."

"Better late than never."

His emotions in turmoil, Edmond said goodbye. His heart went out to Barbara at sixteen, betrayed by their father. And, to some extent, to Mort, who'd been eaten by guilt and just as hurt.

Edmond sat staring at the phone, mulling the implications for himself. He'd been certain after what happened with Barbara that he lacked the instincts for fatherhood. Would he have changed his mind if he'd known the real reason for his sister dropping out of school and moving in with Simon?

Melissa had accused him of deceiving himself about his aptitude as a parent. It hadn't been a deliberate deception, but he might have been blinded by events beyond his control. And with her intuition, she'd understood him at a deeper level.

A noise from the hallway drew his attention.

Dawn stood holding a suitcase, an edge of cloth peeping out where she'd packed in haste. Confused, he said, "Are you planning to spend the night with your friends?"

"No." Only then did he notice her red-rimmed eyes. "I heard you say grandpa isn't sick anymore. Take me back."

Edmond sure hadn't seen this coming. *So much for my fatherly instincts.* "Yes, Grandpa's better, but I'm still your guardian. You're staying with me."

"No." She blinked, her little chest heaving. "I want to go home."

Barely a week ago, he'd have been relieved. Now, giving her up was inconceivable. "I know I'm not the best uncle in the world, but you're my little girl, Dawn."

"Take me home!" she repeated in a fiercer tone. "I don't want to stay here."

Why was she mad at him? "Have I done something wrong?"

"I hate you!" Bursting into tears, the little girl dragged the suitcase back to her room and slammed the door.

Edmond couldn't imagine what had provoked her. Although news of Mort's good health might have prompted the idea of returning to her grandparents, Dawn's reaction seemed excessive. Also, her mood had been subdued ever since they left the animal shelter.

There was a lot at stake, maybe his entire relationship with his niece. He had to keep trying.

Edmond walked down the hall and tapped on her door. "Can I talk to you?"

"Stay out!" she cried. "You're not my father! You don't even like children. You'll be glad when I'm gone."

Every word stung with old truths that no longer held. In the space of a few days with Dawn, Edmond's perception of the world had changed. Sharing breakfast, watching her skip into sports camp each morning to join her new buddies, picking her up and learning about her day—he loved those things. How had he let her down?

He couldn't—wouldn't—return to being the uncle who dropped in once a week to take her to therapy. As Melissa had fought for her babies, he was going to fight for Dawn.

"I'd be miserable if you left," Edmond said through the closed door. "Please let me in."

"You and Aunt Lissa don't need anybody else," came the ragged answer. "Now you can be happy."

What on earth was she talking about? He tried the knob, and found the door locked.

He supposed a stern, old-fashioned father would force the issue. But Dr. Brightman had said defiant behavior was natural, and Dawn's actions weren't placing her in danger. Edmond chose to let it ride and change tactics. "What should I fix for lunch?"

"I'm not hungry."

"Are you kidding? Your stomach's growling so loud, I thought it was thunder."

For a moment, it seemed Dawn might not answer. Then she said, "Peanut butter."

"With jelly or marmalade?"

"I don't care."

"Okay. I'll call you when it's ready." Grateful that she'd spoken to him, Edmond went to fix lunch.

He'd have to play this by ear. Edmond hoped he'd developed some essential paternal sensitivity, even if it hadn't come naturally.

"IT'S ALMOST LIKE cheating." Reaching the bottom of the steps, Melissa set the lock on the chair lift and eased out of the seat.

"Cheating?" Karen planted hands on hips. "With you and Zora both pregnant, I'm glad I didn't remove this after Mom died." She'd installed the device while caring for her mother, who'd battled Parkinson's disease.

She had to admit, having an easy way to go up and down—including a remote that allowed her to summon the seat should Zora leave it on the other floor—would be invaluable.

"You're wonderful," she told her friend. "I'd be lost without you."

"What am I, chopped liver?" Rod demanded, descending from above, where he'd posted himself to keep an eye on Melissa's maiden journey.

"Thank you, too." She gave him a weary smile.

Following last night's altercation with the Grants and her blowup at Edmond, Melissa hadn't slept well. A short while ago, when Edmond had called, she'd assumed for a moment he might be willing to discuss their quarrel. Instead, he'd had more pressing issues on his plate.

He'd filled her in about Mort's depression and the reason for it. Although she was glad the older man wasn't suffering from dementia, the revelation about his brutality to Barbara turned Melissa's stomach—and Edmond's, too, she gathered. He'd also mentioned Dawn's rebellion but assured her he would figure out the cause on his own. With no further comments, he'd ended the call.

She missed being on his team. On Dawn's team, too. But

it seemed her outburst last night had permanently closed that door.

"Something wrong?" Karen asked.

Melissa had no intention of mentioning either her quarrel with Edmond or his father's revelation. Since her friend already knew about her other problem, she focused on that. "I'm worried about what to do if the Grants get me fired."

"I'll organize a protest." Karen accompanied her to the kitchen to start lunch. "I remember when they proposed giving you the embryos, how uncertain you were and how much they pressured you."

Nevertheless, Melissa doubted that would save her job. "I suppose I could find a laboratory position like I used to have. But I'd hate to give up working with our clients and my friends on the staff."

"Screw that," Rod said.

Karen glared at him. "Language!"

"Sorry." Rod didn't appear regretful, though. "Being around my daughters last night reminded me how important it is to fight for what you love, even if you lose. They know how much I love them because they understand how far I was willing to go."

"I *do* intend to fight," Melissa responded heatedly. "I'm talking about accepting the loss of my job, not giving up my daughters."

Karen raised her hands. "I'm declaring a moratorium on arguments, spats, quarrels…"

"We weren't quarreling," Rod said.

"Much," Melissa qualified.

"And sharp tones of voice," Karen finished. "Okay, what kind of sandwiches does everyone want?"

"Depends on what's available." From the fridge, Rod extracted bread, cold cuts and condiments.

Melissa pitched in. Yet the moment she let her thoughts wander, they fixed on another kitchen a few miles away.

What were Edmond and Dawn discussing over lunch? Had he uncovered the source of her rebellion?

For three years, Melissa had believed that her ex-husband had been wrong for her and that her closeness to him had vanished forever. Then, these past weeks, experiencing his tenderness, his devotion to his niece and his concern for his sister and parents, she'd let down her guard. No, she'd gone far beyond that. She'd fallen in love with him again.

But however she might feel about him, her loyalty to her daughters came first.

EDMOND HAD HOPED Dawn would emerge from her room for lunch in better spirits. Instead, the little girl stared down at her plate throughout the meal, although she did consume most of her sandwich and several cream-cheese-filled celery sticks, She responded to his questions in monosyllables.

As soon as she was done, Dawn grabbed her camera and scraped open the rear sliding door, avoiding Edmond's gaze as she darted out. While she hadn't repeated her insistence on leaving, neither had she unpacked her suitcase, he noted when he peered into her room.

Edmond considered placing an emergency call to Dr. Brightman. However, he wasn't ready to admit failure.

After cleaning up the lunch dishes, he glanced out the window. Dawn's small figure prowled through the bushes at the rear of the lot, halting as she spotted something. He adjusted his glasses and then he saw it, too, a flash of emerald hovering in front of an orange trumpet-shaped flower. A hummingbird.

How magical, and how endearing he found his niece's fierce concentration as she took aim. Lowering the camera, she continued to watch the tiny bird.

I can't give her up. Especially after what he'd learned about his father. Not that his dad was likely to hit her, but

Edmond could never entrust Dawn to them. She was his child now.

Still, he had no clue why she was pushing him away. Since he was batting zero on that, he decided to seize this chance, with Dawn out of earshot, to call the Grants. Stiffening his composure, he pressed their number.

Nell answered. After greeting him, she said, "Vern's not home."

"Can we just talk?" Through the window, he watched Dawn. She'd moved on to investigate a neglected flower-bed where a few scraggly marigolds lingered. "This needn't be formal."

"I suppose it's all right. Hold on." In the background, a baby was crying. A minute later, the wailing stopped, and then Nell spoke again. "Okay, I'm settled."

"How did you feel about last night's discussion?" Edmond said.

Nell sighed. "I was picturing her the way she used to be, smooth and in charge. So it came as a shock to witness a different side of her."

Unsure of her mood, he framed his response with care. "She caught me off guard, too."

"I understand how uncomfortable and scary it is to carry triplets," Nell said. "I can't blame her for being upset."

"She'd do anything for those kids," Edmond said. "And I'd do anything to help her." He hadn't registered until he spoke how strongly he meant that.

"How do *you* feel about babies?" she asked.

"Me?" Tricky subject. "I don't have much experience."

"Ever hold one?"

"My niece." Edmond responded, instantly hit by a sweet memory of her baby scent and wide-eyed gaze.

"How did you react?" Nell probed.

"I was afraid I'd drop her." Edmond chuckled. "She's

seven years old now, and I haven't dropped her yet." Firmly, he steered back on course. "About the triplets…"

"I guess it was unrealistic to hope she'd accept our terms." Nell's frankness made him want to stand up and cheer. But they hadn't won yet.

"I'd hate for Melissa to land in trouble at work," Edmond said. "But she's the mother of those triplets, and she'd put her life on the line for them, let alone her job."

"How about you?"

The woman had a talent for throwing curve balls. "Excuse me?"

"How do you feel about these babies, specifically?"

He might as well be frank. "I'm still growing into the reality of being a father, but it's astonishing. Transformative. Utterly unique…" The words choked off as he recalled Dawn's anger. What if he *couldn't* figure out what was wrong with her?

"I understand," Nell said. "Vern and I will talk this over and call you again."

"Thanks." Edmond waited in case she had more to say, but she clicked off.

Only then did it occur to him that she'd misinterpreted his comments about fatherhood. He'd been referring to Dawn, not the triplets. Hadn't he?

The screen door slid open. "Who was that?" Dawn asked. "Why were you talking about the babies?"

Damn. He'd forgotten to keep an eye on her and protect her from this conversation. Too late, and if he lied, she'd sense it. Moreover, he'd be setting a bad precedent. "It was the donor mommy of Aunt Lissa's babies. We were just discussing—"

Her face crumpled. "Don't give away my sisters!"

"What on earth?" Surely she hadn't drawn that conclusion from anything he'd said. "Where'd you get that idea, Dawn?"

She scuffed her shoe against the floor. "If I tell you, will you promise I can still play with them?"

"Amber and Tiffany?"

A short nod confirmed his guess.

"Of course you can play with your friends, whenever they're available." Edmond reached for his niece and, hesitantly, she scooted closer. "What did they say?"

"They heard Karen and Rod talking at their grandma's house." The story spilled out—the Adams girls had believed the babies might be given away to save Melissa's job. Tears rolled down her cheeks.

Distressed, Edmond lifted Dawn onto his lap. "That's the problem with gossip. It doesn't give you the whole story. Aunt Lissa and I hate this idea. It didn't come from us and we're fighting it."

"You used to not want children." She must have heard that from Barbara. Or maybe she was remembering something he'd said during the divorce, he thought remorsefully.

"That was a long time ago. People change," Edmond said. "I have, a lot. I'd never been a father before. You're teaching me all sorts of important things."

His niece sniffled. "You wouldn't be happier if it was just you and Aunt Lissa?"

"I'd be terribly sad without my little Dawn," he assured her gruffly. "Nobody's giving anybody away. Not you, and not the triplets."

Her cheek rested against his shoulder. "You promise?"

"I'm not letting anyone take you. We're a family." His chest hurt from the swell of emotions. "As for the babies, they're family, too. And so is your aunt."

Could he honestly claim to be Melissa's family, especially after their argument? But he was. He'd never stopped loving her, no matter how hard he'd tried over the years. He couldn't bear to lose her again, or Dawn, or those three little girls who had become real to him before he knew it.

How ironic that, for so long, he'd carried the guilt of failing his sister. Although he still didn't fully understand why Barbara hadn't confided in him, he no longer believed that her actions were his fault.

And he no longer believed he was hopeless as a father. Today, he'd been sensitive enough to elicit the cause of Dawn's unhappiness.

No wonder Melissa had been frustrated at his refusal to acknowledge his fatherly instincts. He had plenty of them. That left the hard part: what was he going to do about it, and about their disagreement?

What's your best and worst case scenario? No, scratch that. What's your goal?

Suddenly, his path became obvious. "I have an idea," Edmond said. "But I need your help."

"Okay, Daddy." Snuggling against him, Dawn didn't seem to notice the endearment she'd used.

Although Edmond suspected he might not hear that term often, it marked an important step. That was how love grew, he was discovering. Sometimes gradually, in fits and starts, and sometimes in a big leap.

He was ready for a leap. "Let's get started."

Chapter Nineteen

"I should have remembered not to play Scrabble with you." Zora studied the board with disgust. "You always win."

"I had lucky draws." Collecting the tiles for storage, Melissa smiled at the picture they made, sitting at the table barely able to reach the board due to their swollen bellies. "We may not be able to play again for a while. My arms won't stretch that far."

Draped over an armchair in the den, Lucky glanced up from his computer tablet. "We ought to measure you guys to see who's bigger."

"Who cares?" Zora shot back.

"It would be in the interest of science," Lucky continued. "Twins due in three months versus triplets due in four."

"Our doctors already have that information." Melissa had no desire to turn their pregnancies into a contest.

"Also, Melissa's two inches taller than Zora," Karen observed from the couch. "That might affect the results."

"It's an interesting idea, though," Rod murmured from beside her as he lowered his medical journal. "Considering that we're all sitting around like dullards on a Saturday afternoon."

"Exactly." Lucky ran a hand over his short dark hair. "My old roommates would have placed bets."

"Your old roommates were slobs," Zora said.

"But never boring."

A phone rang. Everyone reached for pocket or purse before pausing in recognition of the ring tone. It was Melissa's.

Her heart skipped at the name on the readout. "Edmond," she answered. "What's up?"

"Any chance your friends could babysit Dawn for a while?" He spoke with a cheerful lilt. "I'll bribe them by bringing dinner."

"If you're bringing dinner, why do you need them to babysit?" Melissa asked.

"You and I are going out," he said.

"Is that how you ask for a date these days?" she teased, grateful for his willingness to reach out to her.

"We have a few things to discuss," Edmond responded lightly. "Okay?"

"Sure." Never mind that those things might be uncomfortable, as long as they were friends again. "How's Dawn?"

"Much better. I ferreted out what upset her." He explained about Rod and Karen's indiscreet remarks and Dawn's conclusion that children—both her and the babies—were expendable.

"That's horrible." Around the room, everyone was trying to appear busy, all the while listening so hard their ears must hurt. "I'd be happy to join you for dinner."

"Give me an hour, okay?" he said. "Oh, and is it okay if Dawn shoots pictures in your yard? The Gladstones' book inspired her."

"You bet. We have plenty of bugs, birds and so on. See you in an hour." Ending the call, she took a deep breath, ignoring the curious looks from her friends.

Edmond was ready to talk. A twinge of fear warned that he might be planning to withdraw further, yet if so, why the upbeat tone? Belatedly, she recalled that he hadn't mentioned the Grants. Had he phoned them yet?

Their unreasonable demands had wrecked her night's

sleep and the fallout had hurt Dawn, too. Much as she'd rather skip chastising Rod and Karen, their gossiping had added to the problem.

In the past, Melissa would have avoided the confrontation, but now she'd learned it was better to address the issue. Firmly, she faced the couple on the couch. "Remember the rule about not discussing any of our personal business around others?" she began.

PARKING HIS SEDAN in the driveway, Edmond recalled his first visit to the blue-trimmed white house. Had the wedding been only a month ago? Since then, his entire life had changed.

And he intended to change it much more. "Well, kid?" he asked Dawn.

She clutched her camera. "Ready for action, Uncle Eddie."

"This is a fantastic place to take photos."

"I can't wait to show them to Mia." School started on Monday and, although her friend was a year older, Paula Humphreys had assured Edmond the girls could sit together at lunch. She'd also arranged, at his request, for Dawn to be in her class.

He retrieved two of the three large sacks he'd bought at Papa Giovanni's. The aromas of tomato sauce, oregano, garlic and other spices covered the familiar scent of the estuary.

In the driveway, Dawn placed her hand into the crook of his arm. "We're a team, aren't we, Uncle Eddie?"

"Now and forever," he said.

SINCE MELISSA'S CHILDHOOD, the glory of the sun setting over the ocean had delighted her. Tonight, as golden and scarlet streaks transformed the western sky above Safe Harbor into a painter's palette, her spirits soared.

She and Edmond were alone in a small grassy park that divided the harbor from a beach, currently empty of sun-bathers thanks to the nippy evening breeze. With the waves unusually calm, surfers were taking the evening off, as well. Only a few joggers and dog-walkers passed by.

While Edmond spread a cloth over the picnic table, Melissa glanced toward the harbor, where sailboats skimmed toward their moorings. At this hour, the swimwear and surfboard shops along the quay had closed, although the Sea Star Café was serving food outdoors beneath warming lamps, an ironic touch considering that it was August. Melissa welcomed the cool breeze.

"Comfortable?" Edmond removed containers of food from a large sack. "Sorry about the hard bench."

"No worries. That smells divine," she said. "This is a treat."

"For me, too." On paper plates, he served a pesto dish along with salad and bread, and sparkling grape juice in plastic glasses.

He'd been gracious earlier with her housemates, Melissa reflected. Karen and Rod had apologized for their negligence. They'd believed themselves out of the girls' earshot. But they shouldn't have run that risk, they'd admitted.

All's well that ends well, Edmond had said.

Thank you, Karen had responded. *I've learned my lesson.*

Me, too. Rod's face had gone red with embarrassment. For once, he didn't attempt to joke about the situation.

I forgive you, too, Dawn had added. *Just don't do it again.* She'd been in a buoyant mood after the frank discussion with her uncle.

"I'm impressed by how well you and Dawn talk," Melissa told Edmond as they ate.

Fork in hand, he paused to gaze at her, his contact lenses

emphasizing the rich brown of his eyes. "It's astonishing what a difference it makes when people actually listen."

"You've always been an excellent listener." That quality had impressed her from the start.

"I'm a better one now." He cleared his throat. "Which brings me to something I wanted to discuss."

Her phone trilled. Melissa checked the readout. "It's Nell Grant." Anxiety pumped up her heart rate.

Although reluctant to risk spoiling their evening if this were bad news, Melissa couldn't bear to delay. "I'm sorry but I have to take it." Receiving his understanding nod, she answered. "Hi, Nell."

"Hi." The woman hesitated. "I hope I'm not interrupting your dinner, but I promised Edmond this afternoon that I'd call."

"You did?" She was surprised he hadn't mentioned that conversation.

"Vern and I have been reconsidering our position," Nell continued, barely audible above the intermittent rumble of waves. "There's a part of me that will always wish we could have raised our little girls."

Melissa gripped the phone so hard it dug into her hand.

"But your condition reminded me what my pregnancy was like and the reasons I can't go through it again," Nell said. "You're right. You didn't agree to serve as our surrogate. You undertook this pregnancy out of love, and you're their mother now."

Melissa released a long breath. "You won't seek custody?"

"No, and I'm sorry we upset you," Nell said. "It was a knee-jerk reaction, pure emotion and no common sense. Honestly, we're in no position to raise three more infants."

Melissa had to be sure this drama was truly over. "You won't file a complaint with the hospital?"

"You did nothing wrong," Nell conceded. "If you'd refused, we'd have given the embryos to someone else, and there wasn't anyone I trusted more than I trusted you. My dream confirmed what I already knew, that these babies were meant to be yours."

Over the sea, the moon rose above the last wisps of sunset, and it struck Melissa as the most exquisite sight in the universe. *We're safe.* "I'm a little intimidated about what lies ahead, but we'll be fine."

"I'm sure you will, especially now that you've reconnected with your husband," Nell said. "He'll make a terrific father."

Melissa wasn't sure how the woman had drawn that conclusion, but what mattered was that she no longer faced an agonizing battle. "I'm thrilled. Thank you for calling."

"Can we keep the kids in touch, as we planned?" Nell asked. "We could hold a once-a-year reunion between Thanksgiving and Christmas. Our own way of giving thanks."

Melissa doubted she'd ever be completely comfortable with the Grants again, but the children deserved to know their siblings. "We'll figure something out."

"I'll send you an email to confirm what I've said," Nell went on. "You don't have to worry that we'll change our minds."

"I appreciate that." The extra reassurance reminded Melissa of how much she'd always liked the Grants. "Have a great evening."

"You, too."

After clicking off, she recounted the conversation to Edmond as relief seeped through her entire body.

"Congratulations." Tenderness lit his gaze. "You're incredibly beautiful when you're happy. I'd love for you to be happy all the time."

"Me, too." Part of her conversation with the other woman

still puzzled her, though. "Whatever you said to Nell earlier had quite an impact."

"What in particular?"

"She has the impression we've reconciled and that you're ready to be a father." Melissa raised her hands, palms outward. "I don't mean to criticize."

"It's all right." Edmond leaned forward. "The more perspective I gain on the past, the more I want to kick myself."

"That sounds painful."

"Not as painful as the last three years have been," he said. "Do you remember when I proposed to you?"

"Yes, of course." They'd been walking hand-in-hand on the Santa Monica pier at sunset.

"I promised to love and cherish you forever," Edmond mused. "It seemed easy, since we were on the same wavelength in almost every way. That was part of the problem."

"What do you mean?" Melissa had considered harmony to be among their greatest strengths.

"Since we were always in sync, we never learned to handle serious conflict," he explained. "When I got the vasectomy, I assumed that you'd understand what it signified to me."

She'd taken his action as a dictate: my way or the highway. "What exactly did it signify?"

"That what we shared was too precious to risk." Edmond spoke with grave intensity. "When you left, I believed you didn't love me as much as I loved you."

"But I did!"

"I understand that now." From the table, he picked up a manila envelope she hadn't noticed and removed a sheet of paper.

Even at a glance, it didn't resemble a legal document. "What's that?"

It turned out to be a computer-printed picture of them with two-year-old Dawn in front of a Christmas tree. In black ink, someone had drawn three babies, angled as if held in their arms. Each infant had a bow in her hair.

Underneath, Edmond had written in his bold hand: "Marry me again—for keeps. Let's be a family."

Tears sprang to Melissa's eyes. Could he have changed that much? "You're willing to accept my daughters?"

"Our daughters." He moved close, and his arms encircled her. "I don't just accept them—I love them. I'm not sure how it happened, but while I was becoming Dawn's father, I became theirs, too. Raising four children won't be easy, but I'm looking forward to it."

Much as she longed to shout her agreement, it was hard to accept what she'd longed for but never believed could happen. Melissa had to be careful, for all their sakes. "Do you have any idea what lies ahead? The sleepless nights, chaotic schedules, financial sacrifices."

"Sleepless nights? I'm an old pro," Edmond joked, then grew serious. "I'm not sure anyone can be one hundred percent prepared for this kind of situation, but I want to spend my life with you and Dawn and the triplets. There's nothing more important than that." His embrace tightened. "You're the other half of my soul, Melissa. Please marry me."

She leaned against him, her last doubts vanishing. He was the only man she'd ever loved or ever could love, and by some miracle, he loved her, too. "We can skip the fancy ceremony. We had that already and, besides, I can't picture myself waddling down the aisle like a boat in full sail."

Edmond peered down, his eyes narrowing in mock sternness. "No fair, dodging the best part. Let me hear a loud 'Yes, Edmond, I'd love to be your wife!'"

As the sun glimmered below the horizon, it seemed to Melissa that the waves receded and the world grew still. Her voice rang out as clear as a clarion call. "Yes!"

"Yes what?" he prompted.

"Yes, I love you and I'll marry you, and you better not change your mind because I'll never let you go again!"

"Perfect," he said. "That goes double for me."

When he kissed her, his warmth dispelled the chilly air and filled the empty spaces in Melissa's heart forever.

Forever. That was her favorite word.

Chapter Twenty

Edmond and Melissa remarried the first week of September at the historic Old Orange County Courthouse, with Dawn as flower girl, Geoff Humphreys as best man and Karen as maid of honor. A handful of friends, along with Isabel and Mort, joined the festivities.

To Edmond, the intimate ceremony was as special as their elaborate wedding eight years earlier, although he knew Melissa missed her parents. And they both missed Barbara, who'd been maid of honor at their first wedding.

A week later, after submitting paperwork and obtaining approval from the state department of corrections, he took Dawn to the women's prison where her mother had been assigned. Although he wished Melissa could accompany them, the trip would have been too strenuous.

During the hour-long drive, Dawn peppered him with questions. She considered it funny that they weren't allowed to wear blue jeans because that was what prisoners wore, or forest-green pants with tan tops, which would resemble prison guards' outfits.

But at the sprawling facility, she scarcely spoke during the screening process. And when she first spotted her mother in a large room echoing with the conversations of other prisoners and their families, she clung to Edmond.

His sister appeared healthier than she had in court, he

was pleased to note. Her brown hair, free of purple streaks, was neatly brushed and her hollow cheeks had filled out.

"It's me. Mommy," Barbara assured her daughter. "Give me a hug, Dawnie."

The girl ventured out for a quick embrace, then darted back to Edmond. They took seats across a table from Barbara.

"Do you have pictures of the wedding?" she asked.

"Of course." He'd been allowed to bring them, subject to review by the guards.

As Barbara flipped through the half dozen shots, Dawn went to peer over her shoulder. Soon she was chattering away about her new dress and her bouquet.

"You look beautiful," Barbara said. "And Melissa's *very* pregnant."

"I'm going to have three sisters," Dawn crowed, although that was hardly news. They'd written to her mother at length about the triplets and the wedding.

"Sisters?" Barbara frowned. "They're your cousins."

"No! They're my little sisters," her daughter declared.

At the rise in her voice, a guard glanced over. The woman didn't move in their direction, though.

Edmond understood Barbara's instinct to hold on to Dawn as tightly as possible. However, he was glad when she said to him, "They *are* her sisters, aren't they? You and Melissa have to serve as Dawn's parents now. I'll always be her mom, too, but I blew it."

"If I'd had any idea why you left home…" He let the sentence trail off, cautious about discussing the painful topic in front of Dawn. Although Mort had written a letter of apology, Edmond doubted his sister's emotional wounds had healed.

"I should have told you about my fight with Dad, Eddie," his sister said. "I was too embarrassed and too stupid to get the help I needed. Well, I'm getting it now—the hard way."

"What kind of help?" Dawn frowned. "Like Dr. Brightman?"

"Yes, I do receive counseling," her mother said. "Also, while I'm in prison, I can earn a high school equivalency diploma. Maybe an A.A. degree, too. That's the same as two years of college."

"Terrific. That should help you get a job after you're released."

"I'm not sure if anyone will hire a convicted felon, but I'll worry about that later." Barbara cleared her throat. "I guess Mr. Noriega told you I decided against appealing the conviction. My sentence was fair, and I'm not willing to risk a longer term."

"Yes, he did." Edmond hurried on to share news of his own. "The court has approved my permanent guardianship. We passed the family services review with flying colors." The social worker had interviewed him, Melissa and Dawn, as well as conducted a home visit.

He waited uncertainly for Barb's reaction, unsure of how she'd feel about the word *permanent.*

"That means until she's eighteen, doesn't it?" his sister said slowly. "But I can ask to get custody when I'm released."

"Yes, if you have a job and a stable living situation." Despite an effort to sound neutral, Edmond couldn't avoid the edge to his voice. "Once she's twelve, she'll have the right to choose, though."

Dawn stared at them both, lips pressed tightly. Although he'd explained this to her earlier, it was bound to be a sensitive topic.

"You want to keep her, don't you?" Barbara asked.

"Of course."

Sadness shadowing her face, she gazed at her daughter. "I'd rather have her with me, but she needs stability. Dawn, you can stay with Uncle Eddie and Aunt Lissa till you're grown-up if you want to."

"Can I still see you?" Dawn touched her mother's arm.

"Absolutely!"

"I'll bring her once a month while you're here," Edmond promised. That seemed often enough to maintain the relationship while allowing Dawn to adjust to her new home and school.

"Thank you." Barbara sighed. "This is for the best. I'm the one who let her down."

Much as Edmond yearned to disagree, he couldn't.

Barbara steered the subject to their preparations for the babies. The third bedroom, which they'd designated as the nursery, was filling with toys and baby equipment donated or loaned by friends, Edmond said. The Grants had given them many items that their boys had outgrown.

"Will you send pictures when the triplets are born?" Barbara asked wistfully.

"Yes, Mommy," Dawn said. "I'll take them myself."

"You're a natural photographer." A few minutes later, as Barbara hugged them farewell, her eyes glittered with unshed tears. She faced a hard road ahead, Edmond reflected, but she wouldn't walk it alone.

He told her that, quietly, before he left, and his sister smiled.

"CAN'T I CHOOSE one, please?" Dawn wheedled, sitting between Melissa and Edmond on the patio lounger. It was a late afternoon toward the end of September. "Not Bambi or Bunny, I promise!"

"Not Belinda either," Melissa replied gently, with what struck Edmond as admirable patience. She must be very uncomfortable these days, with the triplets growing rapidly. After a few weeks of riding to work with Karen, even that had become a strain, and she'd begun telecommuting on a reduced schedule.

The little girl released a melodramatic sigh. "Okay. But we've been through *all* the books. We have to call them something!"

In Edmond's lap, the international-themed book fell open to a page filled with O's—Omorose, Ophelia, Orma. Moments before, they'd been staring at F's—Fayola, Fritzie and Fulvia. Gently rocking the lounger with one leg, he stifled a yawn. It was the third such volume they'd flipped through this afternoon.

"We could draw names from a hat," he joked.

"No, Uncle Eddie!" Dawn scolded.

"I was kidding."

"Let's rest for a minute and enjoy the sunshine," Melissa said. "Maybe the names will sort themselves out in our brains."

Dawn bounced in her seat. "Flowers!"

"They are beautiful." Melissa beamed at Edmond as she regarded the planter overflowing with petunias. "I'm glad you had them planted."

"So am I." He'd hired a gardener as well as a cleaning service.

Dawn waved her hands impatiently. "I mean how about flower names, like Daisy?"

"Maybe not that particular one, but it's a good idea," Melissa responded.

They ran through floral names, including some that Edmond found on his phone. Most he considered too old-fashioned. Blossom. Chrysanthemum. Poppy. "Alyssa is nice."

"My favorite is Lily," Dawn announced.

"That's pretty," Edmond mused. "It reminds me of Tiger Lily in *Peter Pan*."

"Lily of the valley was my mother's favorite scent." Melissa clapped her hands. "We've picked a name!"

"Lily," Dawn said happily. Edmond was glad she'd been able to propose one of the names.

"One down, two to go," he said. "How about other names starting with L?"

"I'd rather not." Melissa half closed her eyes as he continued rocking the lounger. "The girls will have a hard enough time establishing unique identities without that."

On the lawn, a bird alighted and began pecking industriously. "How about bird names?" Dawn asked. "Like Robin or Jay."

"Pelican?" Edmond joked.

"Flamingo," said Melissa.

"You guys, cut it out." The little girl folded her arms.

Melissa took a deep breath. "Now that I think about it, a name caught my attention in one of the books, but I'm not sure it's right. It isn't a bird name, either."

"Out with it," Edmond commanded.

"Simone," she said.

His jaw tightened. Did she really want to call a baby after Dawn's dad? "Why Simone?"

"I had a high school friend named Simone, an exchange student from France," Melissa explained. "Unfortunately, we lost touch over the years."

"Sih-mone," Dawn pronounced. "It sounds sophisticated." That was one of her favorite new words from a story she'd read.

"It's a variation on Simon…" Edmond pointed out.

Melissa stretched her neck. "That's why I was reluctant."

Dawn drooped. "Never mind."

Her disappointment touched him. Of course she had positive feelings about her dad, too. "It's okay that you loved Simon. He loved you, too."

"I don't want Simone to grow up to be a robber," the little girl said.

Melissa stroked her niece's hair. "She doesn't have to be like him in the bad ways."

"Just the good ones." Dawn studied them hopefully. "Okay?"

Melissa quirked an eyebrow at Edmond. "Do we all agree on Simone?"

He did, actually. "Let's go for it. Naming kids after family is a wonderful tradition."

"Excellent idea," Melissa said. "But we tried that, remember?"

None of their female relatives' names had quite hit the mark. Then Edmond came up with one they hadn't considered. "What about your brother?"

"Jamie." Melissa spoke the name gingerly.

"The little boy who died?" Dawn had heard the story. "It can be a girl's name, too, can't it?"

"You bet." Melissa ran a finger across Edmond's cheek. "It's a wonderful suggestion."

"We each picked a name," their niece observed.

"So we did. Lily, Simone and Jamie," Melissa said. "They're lovely."

The lowering sun and his rumbling stomach reminded Edmond that the dinner hour was approaching. "Who's hungry?"

"Me!" said Dawn.

"Me, too," Melissa chimed in.

"It's lucky I know how to cook." He'd learned a lot these past few months, he reflected as he assisted his wife to her feet. Now he had a heart full of love, a house about to be full of babies, and a box full of recipes.

Hard to say which was more important. Grinning to himself, he slid open the patio door and ushered his family inside.

* * * * *

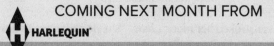